THE

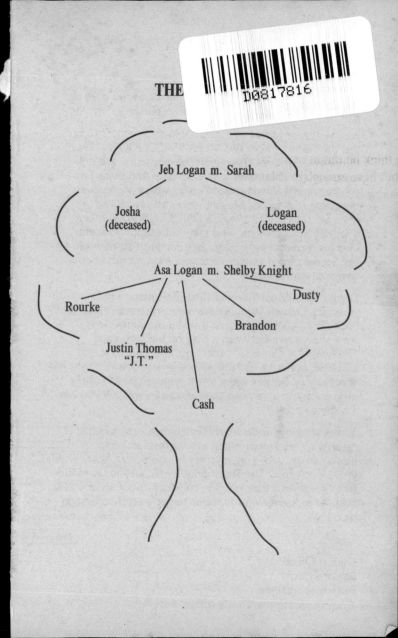

Jeb Logan m. Sarah

Josha
(deceased)

Logan
(deceased)

Asa Logan m. Shelby Knight

Rourke

Dusty

Justin Thomas
"J.T."

Brandon

Cash

Dear Harlequin Intrigue Reader,

To chase away those end-of-summer blues, we have an explosive lineup that's guaranteed to please!

Joanna Wayne leaves goosebumps with *A Father's Duty*, the third book in NEW ORLEANS CONFIDENTIAL. In this riveting conclusion, murder, mayhem…and mystique are unleashed in the Big Easy. And that's just the beginning! *Unauthorized Passion*, which marks the beginning of Amanda Stevens's new action-packed miniseries, MATCHMAKERS UNDERGROUND, features a lethally sexy lawman who takes a beautiful imposter into his protective custody. Look for *Just Past Midnight* by Ms. Stevens from Harlequin Books next month at your favorite retail outlet.

Danger and discord sweep through Antelope Flats when B.J. Daniels launches her western series, McCALLS' MONTANA. Will the town ever be the same after a fiery showdown between a man on a mission and *The Cowgirl in Question?* Next up, the second book in ECLIPSE, our new gothic-inspired promotion. *Midnight Island Sanctuary* by Susan Peterson—a spine-tingling "gaslight" mystery set in a remote coastal town—will pull you into a chilling riptide.

To wrap up this month's thrilling lineup, Amy J. Fetzer returns to Harlequin Intrigue to unravel a sinister black-market baby ring mystery in *Undercover Marriage*. And, finally, don't miss *The Stolen Bride* by Jacqueline Diamond— an edge-of-your-seat reunion romance about an amnesiac bride-in-jeopardy who is about to get a crash course in true love.

Enjoy!

Denise O'Sullivan
Senior Editor
Harlequin Intrigue

THE COWGIRL IN QUESTION

B.J. DANIELS

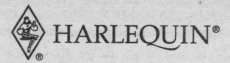

HARLEQUIN®

TORONTO • NEW YORK • LONDON
AMSTERDAM • PARIS • SYDNEY • HAMBURG
STOCKHOLM • ATHENS • TOKYO • MILAN • MADRID
PRAGUE • WARSAW • BUDAPEST • AUCKLAND

I dedicate this book to my editor, Denise O'Sullivan. Thank you for your faith, support and encouragement over the years. It's a privilege to work with you.

ISBN 0-373-22797-3

THE COWGIRL IN QUESTION

Copyright © 2004 by Barbara Heinlein

www.eHarlequin.com

Printed in U.S.A.

ABOUT THE AUTHOR

B.J. Daniels is a former award-winning journalist. Her book *Premeditated Marriage* won *Romantic Times Bookclub Magazine*'s Best Intrigue award for 2002, and she also received a Career Achievement Award for Romantic Suspense. B.J. lives in Montana with her husband, Parker, three springer spaniels, Zoey, Scout and Spot, and a temperamental tomcat named Jeff. She is a member of Kiss of Death, the Bozeman Writers' Group and Romance Writers of America. When she isn't writing, she snowboards in the winters and camps, water-skis and plays tennis in the summers. To contact her, write P.O. Box 183, Bozeman, MT 59771 or look for her online at www.bjdaniels.com.

Books by B.J. Daniels

HARLEQUIN INTRIGUE

312—ODD MAN OUT
353—OUTLAWED!
417—HOTSHOT P.I.
446—UNDERCOVER CHRISTMAS
493—A FATHER FOR HER BABY
533—STOLEN MOMENTS
555—LOVE AT FIRST SIGHT
566—INTIMATE SECRETS
585—THE AGENT'S SECRET CHILD
604—MYSTERY BRIDE
617—SECRET BODYGUARD
643—A WOMAN WITH A MYSTERY
654—HOWLING IN THE DARKNESS
687—PREMEDITATED MARRIAGE
716—THE MASKED MAN
744—MOUNTAIN SHERIFF*
761—DAY OF RECKONING*
778—WANTED WOMAN*
797—THE COWGIRL IN QUESTION†

*Cascades Concealed
†McCalls' Montana

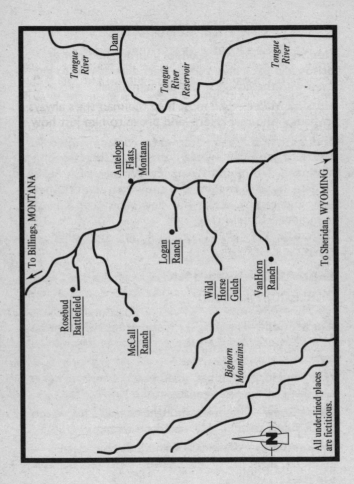

To Billings, MONTANA

Tongue River

Dam

Tongue River Reservoir

Tongue River

Rosebud Battlefield

McCall Ranch

Antelope Flats, Montana

Logan Ranch

Wild Horse Gulch

VanHorn Ranch

To Sheridan, WYOMING

Bighorn Mountains

N

All underlined places are fictitious.

CAST OF CHARACTERS

Rourke McCall—Framed for murder, he's out of prison and back in Antelope Flats determined to get even with the cowgirl who put him in jail.

Cassidy Miller—She must help the man she's always loved find the real killer—and prove to him just how wrong he is about her.

Blaze Logan—She would do anything to get what she wants. But murder?

Forrest Danvers—Was he murdered because he was with the wrong woman? Or did Forrest have another secret that got him killed?

Cecil Danvers—Someone is going to pay for killing his brother and ruining his life.

Easton Wells—He stole Rourke's old girlfriend while Rourke was in prison. But is that the only reason he's running scared?

Asa McCall—The rancher has kept secrets from his family. But now his biggest secret of all is about to come out.

Holt VanHorn—He has a bad habit of stealing things and being in the wrong place at the wrong time.

Gavin Shaw—He never thought he could know too much about anything. He was dead wrong.

Yvonne Ames—She finally wants to come clean about the night of Forrest Danvers's murder. But is it too late?

Prologue

Maybe if Forrest Danvers hadn't been half-drunk or spitting mad, he might have seen it coming.

But then he wasn't expecting any real trouble as he drove up Wild Horse Gulch in the late-night darkness.

The road cut through sheer rock cliffs, then opened to towering ponderosa pines before topping out on a sage-brush-studded bench that overlooked the Tongue River.

Forrest was a little uneasy, given his reason for being there in the first place. Nor did it help that the night was blacker than the inside of a boot and a storm was coming.

But he was feeling too good to go home yet. For the first time in his twenty-one years of miserable life, he felt he could be somebody. Somebody people respected. Not just another one of those no-count Danvers like his brother Cecil.

He parked his pickup on the bench above the river and rolled down his window, feeling closed in, anxious to hear the sound of the other vehicle coming up the narrow mountain road. She was late. As usual. *Women.*

The air had an edge to it, a kind of jittery current that set his nerves on end. He blamed the approaching thunderstorm and the lightning that flickered behind dark bruised clouds at the edge of the horizon.

It promised to be one hell of a storm. In this part of Montana, thunderstorms often swept across the vast open landscape, bringing wind that tore branches from the cottonwoods and rain as large and hard as stones that ran in torrents down the dry creek beds like rivers.

Beyond the closer smell of sagebrush and dust, he picked up the welcome scent of the coming rainstorm. It had been far too hot and dry this summer. The ground needed a good soaking and he needed to cool down in more ways than one.

It had been one hell of a night at the Mello Dee Lounge and Supper Club. At the memory, he flexed his right hand. It hurt like hell, the knuckles skinned and bloody. He smiled at the memory of his fist connecting with Rourke McCall's face.

Forrest could feel his left eye swelling shut. At least the cut over his right had stopped bleeding. That was something. And, he thought taking a shaky breath, his ribs hurt where he'd taken a punch, but Forrest had got in a few good licks himself.

Rourke McCall had just been itching for a fight. Forrest saw that now. Saw that he'd been a fool to oblige the crazy bastard. But what else could he have done? Just let Rourke cut in on the dance floor when Forrest was enjoying himself with Blaze Logan?

That was the problem with Rourke. He thought he owned Blaze, had ever since junior high. What a fool. Anyone with a pocketful of money could have Blaze—at least until the cash ran out.

Forrest rolled a cigarette, lit it and glanced at his

watch before tossing the match to the floorboard. In that instant between light and darkness, he looked out and thought he saw someone silhouetted against the storm.

He stared into the darkness, unnerved until lightning lit the horizon and he could see that there was nothing out there but clumps of silver sage and sun-golden grasses bent to the breeze.

Just the booze playing tricks on him. He crushed out the last of his cigarette, wishing now he'd just gone home. Leaning back, he pulled his cowboy hat down over his face and closed his eyes. He was tired and sore and already feeling a little hungover. This had been a bad idea, but if she'd ever get here...

The night air felt good coming in through his open window. He half listened for the sound of the vehicle coming up the creek road, half dozed.

He'd dropped off into a deep, alcohol-drenched sleep when he was startled awake. At first all he heard was the whine of a vehicle engine coming up the road and the low rumble of thunder. Lightning flickered across the horizon, then died, leaving the night even darker.

But as he listened, he realized that wasn't what had awakened him.

He sat up a little, trying to place the sound. Then he heard it again. The soft scrape of boot leather brushing against sagebrush.

He sat up straight, pushed back his hat and, rubbing his hand over his face to wake up, stared out his open side window into the blackness.

The air seemed to change around him an instant before he saw the barrel of the pistol. Just a glint of blued steel appearing out of the night right next to him and the open window.

He stared at the gun, more than a little startled to realize that he really *wasn't* alone, probably hadn't been for most of the time he'd been sitting there.

He frowned, uncomprehending. In the distance, the sound of the vehicle coming up the road grew closer and closer.

For just a split second, the gun, the gloved hand holding it and the face of the person were illuminated in a flash of lightning. Just long enough for Forrest Danvers to face his killer.

"No!" The deafening boom of the gunshot drowned out his cry. He felt the burning heat as the lead entered his chest. The second shot exploded from the barrel of the gun. He barely noticed it. In the flare of the gunshot, he studied the killer's face, wanting to hang on to every familiar feature until they met again in hell.

Chapter One

Eleven years later

A storm blew in the day Rourke McCall got out of prison.

At the Longhorn Café, Cassidy Miller brushed back an errant strand of hair from her face and tried to pretend it was just another day as she picked up the coffeepot and headed for the table in the corner now full of ranch hands from the VanHorn spread.

On the way, she made the mistake of looking out the window. The sky outside had turned dark and ominous, dust devils swirled in the street, the first drops of rain pelted the front window and streaked the glass.

Past the rain and dust, someone else was also staring out at the storm—and her. Blaze Logan stood at the window of the Antelope Development Corporation. Their eyes met across Main Street and Cassidy felt a chill rattle through her.

"I'll take a little more of that coffee, Cass," called Dub Morgan, the VanHorn Ranch foreman, from the table she'd been heading toward.

Cassidy dragged her gaze away from the window

and Blaze, not realizing that she'd stopped walking, and took the pot of coffee over to the tableful of cowboys. But as she filled their coffee cups and joked and smiled, her mind was miles away in Deer Lodge, Montana, where Rourke McCall, the wildest of the McCall boys, would be walking out the gate of the Montana State Prison this morning.

None of her patrons had mentioned it, but everyone in town knew. That was one reason the café was packed this morning and she'd had to call in an extra waitress.

Everyone was wondering if Rourke would come back to town and make good on the threat he'd made against her eleven years ago.

As he was being dragged out of the courtroom in handcuffs, he had called back to Cassidy, "I know you framed me. I'm going to get out and, when I do, I'll be back for you."

The judge had given him twenty-five years but Rourke was walking out a free man after only eleven. For most of those years, Rourke had worked the prison's cattle ranch. Ironic since he'd hated working the family ranch and done everything possible to avoid it in all the years Cassidy had known him.

Good behavior, the warden had told the parole board. "Rourke McCall is a changed man. A reformed man. He is no longer a threat to society."

No, he was only a threat to Cassidy Miller—no matter what he told the parole board or the warden.

"You okay, honey?" Ellie whispered, slowing as she passed Cassidy with an armload of plates headed for the VanHorn Ranch table.

Cassie nodded and glanced outside again, trying to

imagine what it would be like seeing Rourke after all these years. Maybe he really was a changed man. Maybe he was reformed. Maybe he'd forgotten his threat against her.

But even as she thought it, she knew better. Rourke McCall might have fooled the prison officials but he couldn't fool her.

The bell dinged indicating that an order was up. She moved toward the kitchen, determined to keep up a good front. She didn't want anyone to know she'd been dreading this day for eleven years. Or the real reason why.

ACROSS THE STREET, Blaze Logan stood at the window watching the crowd at the Longhorn Café and smiling to herself. How appropriate that one hell of a thunderstorm would hit town just before Rourke McCall did.

She could sense the change in the air, smell the rain and expectation, hear the hush that had fallen over Antelope Flats, Montana. She loved nothing better than a good knock-down-drag-out fight. She'd had that and more the night Forrest Danvers was murdered and she was ready for the hell Rourke was going to cause when he got back.

As she caught another glimpse of Cassidy Miller through the café window across the street, her smile broadened. Cassidy. The good girl and a thorn in Blaze's side since they were kids. Her cousin Cassidy had always been the perfect one. She now owned her own business, was president of the chamber of commerce, helped with every damned fund-raiser in town. No one ever had a bad word to say about her.

"Why can't you be more like Cassidy," her father had said from as far back as Blaze could remember.

She and Cassidy competed against each other in regional rodeos and Cassidy always won, and Blaze always threw a fit when she lost.

"You could learn something about being a good sport from your cousin," her father would say.

But Blaze knew she should have won, had to win, was expected to win because her great-grandmother had been a trick rider with a Wild West show. Her cousin Cassidy's great-grandmother was nobody.

"Even when Cassidy loses, she's gracious," her father would say.

Yeah, well that was because Cassidy seldom lost at anything.

Except when it came to Rourke McCall. Blaze had felt not even a twinge of guilt when Cassidy had confessed back in junior high that her dream was to someday marry Rourke McCall.

Blaze had never paid much attention to Rourke before that. He was tall, sandy-blond with blue eyes and a temper. At the time, he'd been a teenager, moody and full of himself. She could tell by looking at him even back then that he would never amount to anything.

But Blaze was already developing and boys were noticing. Cassidy, on the other hand, was two years younger, and a tomboy.

Getting Rourke to notice her had been a piece of cake for Blaze, who hadn't really liked him but wanted to win just once. As it turned out, she'd not only beaten Cassidy, she'd ruined any chance her cousin ever had of ending up with Rourke McCall.

Blaze stared across the street, catching glimpses of

Cassidy as she worked. Blaze still resented her. Probably because Blaze's father still threw Cassidy up to her.

The worst fight she'd ever had with her father was over Cassidy.

"My whole life you've compared me to Cassidy," she'd cried. "I'm sick of it. I'm nothing like her and I'm glad."

Her father had nodded ruefully. "No, you're right, you're nothing like your cousin. She's doing something with her life. She doesn't just live off her parents."

"Her daddy ran off and her mother is poor," Blaze had retorted. "We're not."

"*I'm* not," John Logan had snapped. "You, my daughter, are going to get a job and start growing up."

"What are you saying?"

"I'm cutting you off. No more money. You're on your own."

Blaze hadn't been able to believe her ears. She'd always been her father's favorite between her and her stepbrother, Gavin Shaw. How could her father turn against her like this? "You're doing this because of Cassidy."

He just shook his head. "You've always put your cousin Cassidy down, but it wouldn't hurt you to be a little more like her."

Well, Blaze thought wryly, she was damned glad she wasn't Cassidy now. She wouldn't want to be in that woman's shoes for anything. Not today. Not with Rourke getting out of prison and coming back to even the score.

No way was Rourke going to let Cassidy Miller get away with what she'd done to him. Blaze was almost rubbing her hands together in her excitement. Antelope Flats had been too dull for too long, but Rourke McCall was about to change all of that.

Unless *he* was the one who'd changed. Unless all that good behavior that got him released early *wasn't* an act. The thought ruined her day. What if he didn't come back? What if he really had put the past to rest?

No, not the Rourke McCall she'd known, she assured herself. He'd just sold all of that bull to the warden so he could get out early. Good behavior and Rourke McCall...the two had never gone together, she thought smiling again.

Poor Cassidy Miller. Blaze couldn't wait. Finally her cousin was going to get her comeuppance. It couldn't happen to a nicer person.

ROURKE MCCALL WALKED out of Montana State Prison, stopped and, looking up at the wide blue sky, took a deep breath of freedom.

Eleven years. Eleven years of his life.

He heard his little brother get out of the pickup and come toward him. Lowering his gaze from the sky, he took Brandon's outstretched hand and shook it firmly, smiling at the youngest of his brothers. Of his family, only Brandon and their little sister Dusty had kept in touch with him on a regular basis, and Dusty only on the Q.T. since their father had forbidden it.

"You have any plans?" Brandon asked as he led the way to one of the ranch pickups.

Rourke stopped to study the graphic painted on the pickup door. The words Sundown Ranch were printed over the top of the longhorn in a stylized print. New. He liked the old, more simple script that had been on the trucks since his grandfather's time much better, but he was sure that a lot of things had changed in the eleven years he'd been gone.

"I mean, if you don't have any plans, I have a few things going I could let you in on," Brandon said as he opened the driver's side door and climbed behind the wheel.

Rourke got in the passenger side. Yeah, a lot of things had changed. He tried to remember if he'd ever ridden with Brandon, who was only nineteen when Rourke had gone to prison. Rourke had only been twenty-two himself. "What kind of things?"

Brandon smiled. "Moneymaking."

Rourke shook his head and leaned back against the seat, adjusting his cowboy hat. "Thanks, but I have plans."

He could feel Brandon's eyes on him. Unlike the warden, Brandon wouldn't even attempt to give him a pep talk about letting go of the past, starting over, looking at this as a new beginning, forgetting he'd been framed for murder and had just spent eleven years of his life in prison because of it.

He closed his eyes and let the sound of the tires on the pavement lull him. He was free. Finally. Free to do what he'd promised himself he would do all those nights in prison.

He didn't wake up until the pickup left the highway and bumped onto the dirt road. He didn't need to open his eyes to know exactly where they were. He'd been down this road enough times to remember every hill and turn and bump. How many times at night in his prison cell had he lain awake thinking about the day he would drive down this road again?

He opened his eyes and rolled down his window, realizing he'd forgotten the exact smell of the sage, the sun-baked earth and summer-dried grasses, the scent of the cool pines and the creek.

He'd forgotten too how much he loved this land. The red rock bluffs, the silken green of the ponderosa trees etched against the summer blue of the sky or the deep gold of the grass, tops heavy, bobbing in the breeze.

McCall Country. Miles and miles dotted with cattle that had been driven up here from Texas by his great-great-grandfather when this country was foreign and dangerous and full of promise.

His memory hadn't done it justice. White puffs of clouds scudded across a canvas of endless deep blue as the pickup raced along the muddy dirt road, still wet from an earlier rain. Chokecherries, dark as blood, bent the limbs of the bushes along the creek as the summer golden grasses undulated in waves over the rolling hills. And above a narrow draw, turkey buzzards circled, black wings flapping slowly over something dead below.

Rourke fought that old feeling of awe and ownership. He stared out, feeling the generations of men before him who had fought for this land, feeling its pull, its allure and the price of that enticement. No matter how he felt about his old man or how Asa McCall felt about him, Rourke was a McCall and always would be.

The pickup dropped over a rise and he saw it. The Sundown Ranch house. It seemed a mirage shimmering in the afternoon sunlight.

Rourke caught his breath, surprised by the ache in

his chest, the knot in his throat. When he'd left here in handcuffs, he hadn't looked back. Afraid he would never see it again if he did.

"We had a hell of thunderstorm here this morning," Brandon said.

Rourke could feel nervous waves of energy coming off his brother as they neared the ranch. No doubt Brandon was worried about the reception the two of them would get. Rourke doubted Brandon had told their father that he was picking up the first McCall to ever go to prison.

Brandon slowed the truck, pulled up in the yard and parked. Rourke sat for a moment after the engine died just looking at the ranch house, reliving memories, the good mixed with the bad, all treasured now.

The house seemed larger than even he remembered it: the logs more golden, the tan rock fireplace chimney towering above the roofline more majestic, the porch stretching across the entire front of the building, endless.

"I've got some business in town, but I'll catch you later," Brandon said, obviously anxious to get going. "Your pickup's over there. Still runs good. I took care of it for you. Left the keys in the ignition."

"Thanks," Rourke said, looking over at his little brother, and extended his hand. "I appreciate everything you've done and thanks for coming up to get me."

"No problem," Brandon said, shaking his hand, then looking at his watch, fiddling with the band.

Rourke studied his little brother. "You're not in any kind of trouble, are you?"

"No," Brandon said too quickly. "I'm fine."

"These investments you were talking about, they're legal, right?" Rourke asked, seeing something in his brother that worried him.

Brandon fiddled with the gearshift, seeming to avoid his gaze. "Hey, it isn't like that, okay?"

It was something, Rourke thought. Something that equaled trouble, sure as hell. "If you need help for any reason—"

"Stop acting like a big brother," Brandon said, then softened his words. "I'm okay. I can take care of myself."

Rourke climbed out of the truck and Brandon took off in a cloud of dust. He watched him leave, wondering how deep Brandon was in. And to whom.

As the sound of the ranch pickup engine died off in the distance, Rourke heard the front door of the house open, heard the solid thump of boot soles on the pine floorboards and knew before he turned that it would be his father.

Asa McCall had always been a big man, tall and broad and muscular. He'd also always been a hard man, mule stubborn, the undisputed head of the McCall clan, his word the last one.

The years hadn't changed him much that Rourke could see. He was still large, rawboned, still looked strong even at sixty-eight. The hair at his temples was no longer blond but gray, the lines around his eyes a little deeper, the sun-weathered face still granite hard and unforgiving.

They stared at each other as Rourke slung his duffel over one shoulder.

"So they let you out," Asa McCall said, his deep voice carrying across the wide porch.

Rourke said nothing. There was nothing to say. He'd told the old man he was innocent eleven years ago and hadn't been believed. Not Rourke McCall, the wildest McCall.

"Don't worry, I'm not staying," Rourke said. "I just came by to pick up my things."

Asa McCall nodded. Neither moved for a few moments, then Rourke mounted the steps and walked past his father and into the ranch house without a word or a look, torn between anger and regret.

As he stepped through the front door, he saw that nothing had changed from the Native American rugs on the hardwood floors to the western furnishings and huge rock fireplace.

He turned at a sound and was struck by the sight of a pretty young woman coming out of the kitchen. She stopped, her eyes widening. A huge smile lit her face as she came running at him, throwing herself into his arms.

"Rourke," she cried. "Oh, I'm so glad you're back."

He stepped away to hold her at arm's length to study his little sister. "Dusty? I can't believe it."

She'd been six when he'd left, a kid. Now she was a woman, although it was pretty well hidden. She wore boys' jeans, a shapeless western shirt and boots. Her long blond hair was woven in a single braid down her back and a straw cowboy hat hung from a string around her neck. She wore no makeup.

"Dusty?"

Neither had heard the front door open. They both turned to find their father filling the doorway.

"We got fencing to see to," Asa said, and turned, letting the door slam behind him.

Rourke listened to his father's boots pound across the porch. "You best get going. We can visit later. I'll let you know where I'm staying in town."

"You're not staying here?" Dusty cried.

Rourke gave her a look.

"Daddy is so impossible," she said, sounding like the teenager she was. "I swear he gets more stubborn every day."

Rourke could believe that. "Where's everyone else?"

"Cash lives in town. You know he's still the sheriff?"

Rourke nodded.

"J.T. is running the ranch now, but Daddy and I help. Brandon is hardly ever around. J.T. is probably still out riding fence this morning. Did Brandon leave?"

"He said he had business in town," Rourke told his sister.

She nodded and frowned. "I hate to think what kind of business. Daddy says he's headed for trouble and I'm afraid he might be right."

Headed for trouble. That's what Asa used to say about him, Rourke thought.

"I'm so glad you're finally home," Dusty said, and stood on tiptoe to give him a kiss on the cheek before closing the front door behind her.

He watched Dusty join their father out in the yard, watched her walk past the old man. Rourke had to smile, recognizing the familiar anger and stubbornness in the set of her shoulders, the tilt of her head. The old man shook his own head as she sashayed past him, giving him the silent treatment just as she'd done to them all when she was mad as a child.

When Asa finally followed after her, he looked older, almost sad, as if another defiant kid would be the death of him.

Rourke's smile faded as he watched his father follow Dusty to one of the ranch pickups. He stayed there at the window until they'd driven away, then he turned and climbed the wide staircase at the center of the room. At the top, the second floor branched out in two wings. Rourke walked down the wood-floored hallway to his old room at the end of the west corridor. He tried the door, wondering if his stuff had been moved out, the room used for something else.

But as the door swung in, he saw that his room was exactly the same as it had been when he'd left eleven years before. He expected the room to smell musty, at least be covered in dust. But neither was the case. Asa must have had the housekeeper clean it each week. What the hell?

He dropped his duffel on the log-framed bed and looked around, spotting the small straw cowboy hat he'd worn the day he'd won his first rodeo event at the age of seven. His first real chaps, a birthday present for his first cattle drive at the age of nine. His first baseball glove. All gifts from his father, placed on the high shelf Asa had built to store memories.

"In the end, that's what life comes down to," his father had told him the day he'd built the shelf. "Memories. Good and bad, they're all you will ever really own, they're all that are uniquely yours and ultimately all you can take with you."

"You think Mom took memories of us to heaven with her?" Rourke had asked, looking up at his father.

Asa's weathered face had crinkled into a smile, tears in his blue eyes. "She could never forget her kids," he said without hesitation. "Never."

"Or you, Dad. I'll bet she remembers you." It was the one time he'd ever seen his father cry, and only for those few moments before Asa could get turned and hightail it out to the barn.

Rourke walked through the bedroom, past the sitting room, to open the patio doors that led to the small balcony off the back. Stepping out, he gulped the afternoon air, the familiarity of it only making the lump in his throat harder to swallow.

As he looked out across the ranch, he spotted his brother J.T. riding in. Rourke watched him until J.T. disappeared behind one of the red-roofed barns, then he turned and went back inside.

Too many memories. Too many regrets.

He looked up again at the high shelf and all his trophies from first grade through high school for every damned thing from best stick drawing to debate, basketball to bull riding, baseball to target practice. And not a lick of dust on any of them.

He shook his head, not understanding himself any better than he did his father. He'd been wild from the time he could walk, bucking authority, getting in trouble, but somehow he'd managed to excel in spite of it. He got good grades without trying. Athletics came easy as well. In fact, he thought, studying the trophies on the shelf, maybe that was the problem. Everything had always come too easily.

He glanced around the room suddenly wondering why he'd come back here. Not to get his things. He hadn't left anything here he needed. His grandfather had left all of them money, money Rourke had never touched. He could buy anything he needed for this new life the warden had tried to sell him on. He didn't even need his old pickup. Hell, it was fifteen years old.

But he couldn't leave without taking something. He went to the chest of drawers, opened several and took out jeans, underwear, socks, a couple of once-favorite T-shirts he knew he would never wear again and stuffed them into the duffel bag, zipping it closed.

Then he picked up the duffel bag and started to leave the room. His throat tightened again as he turned and spotted the faded photograph stuck in the edge of the mirror over the bureau.

It was a snapshot of Blaze and Cassidy.

He dropped the duffel bag on the bed and walked to the mirror. Blaze with her mass of long, curly fire-engine red hair and lush body standing next to her cousin at the rodeo grounds. Blaze nineteen and full of herself, he thought with a smile.

His gaze shifted to Cassidy and the smile evaporated. Cassidy looked plain next to Blaze with her brown hair and big brown eyes peering out of the shadow of her cowboy hat. Blaze was smiling at the camera, her hat pushed back. She was smiling at him behind the camera, flirting, being Blaze.

But Cassidy was leaning back against the fence, head angled down, peering out at the camera and him from under the brim of the hat, not smiling. Not even close. Her brown eyes were narrowed in an expression he hadn't even noticed. Probably because he'd only had eyes for Blaze.

Now, though, he recognized the expression. Anger. Cassidy Miller had been furious with him.

He swore and plucked the picture from the edge of the mirror, remembering when he'd taken it. Only a week before Forrest Danvers's murder.

Stuffing the photo into the duffel along with the clothes, he zipped it closed again and walked out of the room as he'd done eleven years ago, slamming the door behind him. He'd waited eleven years for this day. He couldn't wait to see Cassidy.

Chapter Two

Cecil Danvers woke that afternoon with the worst hangover of his life. He rolled off the soiled cot he called a bed and stumbled to the rusted refrigerator for his first beer of the day.

He'd downed most of the can when he remembered what day it was. He stood in front of the fridge, listening to it running, waiting for the sweet feel of justified anger.

For the past eleven years, he'd plotted and planned for this day, but now that it was here, he had trouble working up the murderous rage he'd spent years nurturing.

Rourke McCall was to blame for every bad thing that had happened to him since the night his brother Forrest was murdered.

A lot of people in the county didn't understand; they just thought Cecil was lazy, that he'd lived off Forrest's death all these years. They just didn't understand what it had been like to lose his only little brother, especially one who'd always taken care of him.

Cecil finished his beer, burped loudly and smashed the can in his fist before hurling it toward the trash can.

No matter what anyone said, he knew his life would

have been better if Forrest had lived. He certainly wouldn't be living in this rat hole on the tiny patch of land his mother had left him, living in the old homestead cabin that was falling down around his ears.

Nope. Forrest would have seen that he was taken care of. After all, Forrest was the smart one, the strong one. Hadn't their old man always said so?

"Forrest is going to make something of his life," the old man would say. "And if you're lucky, Cecil, he'll take care of your sorry ass as well."

Now he had no one, Cecil thought as he opened the fridge and downed another beer, his eyes narrowing, stomach churning. His father had died right after Forrest's murder. A farming accident. Happened all the time. Cecil's mother hadn't been far behind him. She was always moping around, crying over Forrest as if Forrest had been her only son.

Cecil shoved the memories away and concentrated on Rourke McCall. Yep, if it hadn't been for Rourke, Cecil wouldn't be forced to work when he ran out of money, mucking out other people's horse barns or swabbing the local bars after hours.

He downed the rest of the beer, crushing the can in his fist and throwing it in the general·direction of the trash can. Everyone in town was going to say that Rourke McCall had paid his debt to society for killing Forrest.

They'd tell Cecil to forget it, just as they had for the past eleven years. But people had always underestimated him, he thought grimly. He was the last of his family. It was up to him now. Rourke McCall had ruined his life and Cecil wasn't about to let him get away with it.

ROURKE HAD JUST PUT his duffel on the seat of his pickup and was about to climb in when he saw his brother J.T. lead a large bay mare into the barn.

"Might as well get it over with," he said under his breath, and walked toward the barn.

J.T. looked up as Rourke entered the cool darkness of the horse barn. The smell of horseflesh and leather, hay and manure filled his senses, sending him back to those cold mornings when he was barely old enough to walk. He and his father would come out here.

Asa would saddle up a horse, then lift Rourke in one strong arm and swing up into the saddle. Together they would ride fence until long after the dew on the grasses dried, the sun rising high and warm over the ranch and the sound of the breakfast bell pealing in the air.

Rourke breathed in the memory as he watched his brother unsaddle the bay, more recent memories of the prison barn trying to crowd in.

"Rourke," J.T. said, looking up as he swung the saddle off. "Welcome home. So you're back."

He'd heard more heartwarming welcomes. "Thanks."

His brother studied him. "You staying?"

He shook his head.

J.T. made a face and started to walk past him.

"The old man doesn't want me here. Remember? He disinherited me. I'm not his son anymore."

J.T. sighed, stopped and turned. "He was upset. He didn't even do the paperwork. You aren't disinherited. You never were."

Rourke tried to hide his surprise.

"You know how he is," J.T. continued. "Says things when he's mad that he doesn't mean."

"Yeah, well, I just saw him and I didn't get the impression he'd changed his mind."

"He also can't say he's sorry any better than you can," J.T. said.

Rourke had been compared to his father all his life. He hated to think he might really be like Asa McCall. As if he didn't have enough problems.

"I assume you heard he had a heart attack," J.T. said. "He can't work the ranch like he used to. I'm doing the best I can with Buck's help, hiring hands for branding, calving and moving cattle to and from summer range. But Dad's going to kill himself if his sons don't start helping him."

Buck Brannigan was a fixture of the ranch. Once the ranch foreman, he was getting up in age and probably didn't do any more than give orders.

Rourke looked out the barn door, squinting into the sunlight. "Dad would rather die working than rocking on the porch. Anyway, he's got other sons."

J.T. swore. "I'd hoped you might settle down, move back here and help out."

Rourke shook his head. "Even if the old man would let me, I'm not ready right now."

"You're determined to stir it all back up, aren't you?"

"Someone owes me eleven years," Rourke said.

"Well, even if you do prove that you were framed, those years are gone," J.T. said. "So how many more years are you going to waste?"

"I didn't kill Forrest."

"Don't you think Cash tried to find evidence that would have freed you?" J.T. demanded. "Hell, Rourke, a team of experts from the state marshal's office were down here for weeks investigating this case, but you think that, after eleven years, you're going to come home and find the killer on your own?" J.T. shook his head in disgust, turned and walked off.

Not on his own. He was going to have help, he thought as he rubbed the mare's muzzle and thought of Cassidy Miller. He'd kissed her right here in this barn when she was thirteen.

Another memory quickly replaced it. Cassidy on the witness stand testifying at his trial.

"SO THE DEFENDANT READ the note that had been left on his pickup windshield and then what did he do?" the prosecutor, Reece Corwin, had asked her.

Cassidy hesitated.

"Remember you are under oath. Just tell the truth."

Rourke could see that she was nervous, close to tears. Her gaze came to his, then skittered away.

"He dropped the note, opened his pickup door, got in and drove away," she said.

"Oh, come on, Miss Miller, didn't the defendant ball up the note, throw it down, jerk open his pickup door so hard it wouldn't close properly the next day and didn't he drive out of the bar parking lot spitting gravel? Didn't he almost hit several people coming out of the bar?"

"Objection!" Rourke's lawyer, Hal Rafferty, had cried, getting to his feet. "He's telling her what to say."

"Overruled. We've heard this from other witnesses. Answer the question," the judge instructed Cassidy. "And Mr. Corwin, please move on."

"Yes," Cassidy said, voice barely audible.

"And what did you hear him say before he left?" the

prosecutor asked. This part was new. This part would put the nail in Rourke's coffin.

Cassidy licked her lips, her eyes welling with tears as she looked at Rourke. "He said, 'I'll kill you, Forrest.'"

"Speak up, Miss Miller."

"He said, 'I'll kill you, Forrest.' But he didn't mean it. He was just—"

"Thank you. No more questions."

Cassidy had left out one important point his lawyer had been forced to remind her of on cross-examination.

"Who wrote the note that was left on my client's pickup windshield, Miss Miller?" Hal Rafferty had asked.

Again tears. "I did."

"And what did that note say?"

Cassidy twisted her hands in her lap, eyes down. "Blaze is meeting Forrest up Wild Horse Gulch."

"You *sent* my client to the murder scene?" Rafferty demanded.

"Objection. There was no murder scene until your client got there."

"Sustained."

"Why did you write that note, Miss Miller?" the attorney demanded.

She stared down at her hands, crying now, shaking her head.

"What did you hope to gain by doing that?" Rafferty asked.

Again a head shake.

"Answer the question, Miss Miller," the judge instructed.

"I don't know why I did it."

"Did someone instruct you to do it?" the attorney asked.

Her head came up. Rourke saw her startled expression. "No. I...just did it on impulse. I thought he should know what Blaze was...doing."

"You a friend of Rourke McCall's?"

She looked at Rourke, then the attorney, and shook her head.

"You were just trying to do him a favor?" the attorney asked. "Or were you trying to set him up for a murder?"

"No." Cassidy had burst into tears. She'd been just a girl, sixteen going on seventeen, shy and gangly. The jury hadn't believed that anyone like Cassidy Miller could have set him up.

"Who put you up to it?" the attorney demanded. "Who?"

"No one did."

But Rourke knew better. Cassidy had left the note. He would never have gone up to Wild Horse Gulch if she hadn't. He wouldn't have been framed for murder.

What he didn't know was why. Or who'd put her up to it.

But he was finally out of prison, finally back, and he was finally going to get the truth out of Cassidy Miller.

AS THE AFTERNOON DRAGGED ON, Blaze Logan found herself pacing in front of the Antelope Development Corporation window or ADC as it was known around the county.

"Sit down, Blaze," Easton Wells finally snapped. "You're making me nervous as hell."

She turned from the window to look at her boss. Easton Wells was thirty-nine, a little old for her in more ways than the nine years between them. He had dark hair and eyes, not bad-looking but nothing like Rourke McCall. Nothing at all. And that was part of Easton's charm. He had a good future, was divorced—no alimony or children, his ex-wife on another continent and not coming back, and Easton thought Blaze was the hottest thing going.

What could she say? She loved it.

But he didn't want to marry her. Not yet, anyway.

"What if Rourke doesn't come back to town?" she lamented out loud.

"I wouldn't blame him," Easton said, not looking up from the papers on his desk. ADC was small, a reception area and the larger office that she and Easton shared.

Blaze shifted her focus from across the street to her own reflection in the large front window. She turned to get a side view, liking what she saw, but she wasn't getting any younger. She was thirty. Almost thirty-one! She needed to think about marriage. And soon. And Rourke's getting out of prison had given her the answer.

"Rourke will bring a little life to this town," she said, trying to get a rise out of Easton. "I, for one, think the diversion will be good. I know I'm getting tired of the status quo."

Easton looked up and shook his head. "I know what you're trying to do and it isn't going to work."

"What?" she asked innocently. She'd been dating Easton for years now off and on. Believing a woman should always keep her options open, she'd also seen

Sheriff Cash McCall a few times. She'd had to initiate the impromptu dates with Cash. Like all the McCalls, he was stubborn and dense as a post. She'd had to practically throw herself at him to even get him to notice her.

Easton wasn't dense. He just didn't want to get married again. But she intended to change that. And Rourke was going to help her. He just didn't know it yet.

"You're trying to make me jealous," Easton said.

She smiled and stepped over to his desk, placed both palms down on the solid oak surface and leaned toward him, making sure her silk blouse opened at the top so he got a tempting view of the cleavage bursting from her push-up bra.

"East, we both know there isn't a jealous bone in your body," she said in her most seductive voice.

He looked up, halting on the view in the V of her blouse appreciatively before looking up into her face.

"It would be a mistake to fool with Rourke," he said, looking way too serious. That was another problem with Easton. He took everything too seriously, like work. He often got mad at her because she was late in the mornings or took too long at lunch or didn't finish some job he'd given her or spent too much time on the phone.

"If I were you, I'd steer clear of Rourke," Easton said.

"Would you?" she asked, lifting a brow as she studied him. "Why, East, you and Rourke used to be best friends."

He nodded. "A long time ago. I'm sure Rourke has changed. I know I have."

Not for the better necessarily, Blaze thought.

"I think you're just mad at Asa. You wouldn't even

be in business if he'd gotten his way." Asa had campaigned with all his power and money against coal-bed methane drilling in his part of Montana. "But you beat him."

Easton shook his head. "Asa McCall is never beaten. All I did was make an enemy of him, which is a very dangerous thing to do."

"And just think how much money you've made because of it," she purred.

"Like I said, I wouldn't mess with any of the McCalls if I were you. You don't want that kind of wrath brought down on you."

She studied him, a little surprised. Easton didn't scare easily. "You make it sound as if the McCalls have done something to you."

"I just wouldn't want any of them to have a reason to come gunning for me," Easton said.

Blaze straightened, a frown furrowing her brows. "Is there any reason Rourke would come after you?"

He looked up at her. "Don't you have work to do?"

"If anyone should fear Rourke it's my cousin Cassidy," she said, going over to the window to look out at the Longhorn Café again.

"You aren't on that kick again." He groaned. "You can't believe that Cassidy set him up for murder."

"Does it matter if she did or didn't as long as Rourke *thinks* she did?"

"It might to Rourke," Easton said behind her. "You're counting on him being that hothead who left here. But it's been eleven years, Blaze. He isn't going to come back the same man who left. He just might surprise you. Instead of going off half-cocked, he might have had time to figure out some things about the night Forrest was murdered."

"You think Rourke is going to blame *me?*" She let out a laugh and turned to look at him. "Rourke was crazy in love with me."

"*Was* being the key word here," Easton said without looking up at her.

She glared daggers at him. "I take it back. I think you *are* jealous. Or afraid that Rourke might find out something about you. Let's not forget that you're sleeping with me now. Are you worried that Rourke won't like that?"

Easton laughed without bothering to look up. "I think Rourke probably learned his lesson with Forrest."

"What does *that* mean?" she demanded.

"It means Rourke won't be killing any more men who you've slept with. Anyway, where would he start?" Easton laughed.

She continued to glare at him, but he didn't look up. "Let's not forget that you were at the Mello Dee too the night Forrest was murdered."

Easton finally looked up at her, his eyes dark. "Yes, I witnessed the way you work men, Blaze. I saw how you got Forrest to dance with you to make Rourke jealous. I know how you operate."

He was making her angry, but she hated to show it, hated to let him know that he was getting to her. She also didn't like the fact that he thought he knew her. In fact, was wise to some of her methods when it came to men.

"You're afraid of Rourke," she challenged, wondering if she'd hit a nerve or if it was just simple jealousy.

"Is there something you wanted to tell me about that night?"

Easton shot her a pitying look. "I had no reason to kill Forrest Danvers. Can you say the same thing?"

"I couldn't kill anyone," she cried, but right now the thought of shooting Easton did have its appeal.

"Take my advice," he said, going back to the work at his desk. "Stay away from Rourke. It isn't going to make me jealous, but it might make you regret it."

"That almost sounds like a threat."

"I'm trying to save you from yourself, Blaze," he said with a bored sigh. "But I'm not sure anyone can do that."

Blaze turned her back on him again, wondering what she saw in the man. Little, other than what he could afford her, she told herself. And he'd always wanted her. No matter what he said, he'd been jealous of her and Rourke.

She turned her attention back to the Longhorn Café and her cousin Cassidy.

Easton was right about one thing. Blaze *had* danced with Forrest to make Rourke jealous—and to see what he would do. She hadn't expected Forrest to fight him. Nor had she expected Rourke to kill Forrest up at Wild Horse Gulch. At least that was her story and she was sticking to it.

But what if Rourke wasn't that hotheaded bad boy McCall anymore? She hated to imagine. No, Rourke would come back hell-bent over the past eleven years he'd spent in prison, and he'd make a show of looking for the "real" killer, then he'd go berserk one night and end up back in prison. He wouldn't be here long enough to find out much of anything about the night Forrest was murdered.

She realized she could make sure of that—once she and Rourke took up where they'd left off. She would keep him so busy he would have little time to be digging into the past. And that way she'd know exactly what Rourke was finding out about the night Forrest was murdered. She'd make sure he didn't find out anything she didn't want him to. He wasn't messing up her future. She'd see to that.

She caught a glimpse of a pickup she remembered only too well from years ago. Her pulse jumped. Rourke McCall. That pickup brought a rush of memories as Rourke drove slowly up Main Street.

As the pickup passed her window, all she saw of him was his silhouette, cowboy hat, broad shoulders, big hands on the wheel, but there was no doubt about it. Rourke was back in town.

She waved excitedly, but unfortunately he was looking in the direction of the Longhorn Café—and Cassidy. Blaze let out an unladylike curse.

Wasn't this what she wanted? Rourke back? Rourke set on getting even with Cassidy? But just the thought of Rourke interested in Cassidy for any reason set her teeth on edge.

"What?" Easton said impatiently behind her.

She turned to smile at him. "Rourke. He's back."

Easton couldn't have looked more upset and she realized she had him right where she wanted him. Soon she'd have Rourke where she wanted him, too.

If Easton didn't ask her to marry him by the end of the week then her name wasn't Blaze Logan.

But as she looked at her future fiancé, she had a bad feeling he was hiding something from her.

HOLT VANHORN PICKED UP one of his father's prized bronzes from the den end table and hefted it in his hand. The bronze was of a cowboy in chaps and duster, a bridle in his hand as if headed out to saddle his horse, his hat low on his head, bent a little as if against a stiff, cold breeze. Holt had little appreciation for art. What interested him was the fact that the bronze was heavy enough to kill someone.

"Holt?"

He turned, surprised he hadn't heard his father come into the den. Mason VanHorn was frowning and Holt realized his father's gaze wasn't on him but on the bronze Holt had clutched in his fist.

He put down the work of art carefully, avoiding his father's eye. For his thirty years of life he'd been afraid Mason could read his thoughts. It would definitely explain the animosity between them if that were the case.

"So what brings you out to the ranch, Junior?" Mason asked as he walked around his massive oak desk to sit down.

Holt heard the bitterness behind the question. Mason had never gotten over the fact that his only son hated ranching and if he could get his hands on the land, would subdivide it in a heartbeat and move to someplace tropical.

Holt had moved off the ranch as soon as he could, living on the too-small trust fund his grandfather had left him and what few crumbs Mason had thrown him over the years.

His father didn't offer him a chair. Or a drink. Holt could have used the drink at least.

Mason VanHorn was a big man, broad-shouldered with black hair streaked with gray, heavy gray brows over ebony eyes that could pierce through you faster and more painfully than a steel drill bit.

Holt looked nothing like his father, something that he knew Mason regretted deeply. Instead, Holt had taken after his mother, a small, frail blond woman with diluted green eyes and a predilection for alcohol. His mother had been lucky, though. The alcohol had killed her by fifty. At only thirty, Holt didn't see an end in sight. At least not as long as his father kept the purse strings gripped in his iron fist.

"I need to go away for a while." Holt's voice broke and he saw his father's startled expression.

"Away where?" Mason asked.

Holt shook his head. The massive desk was between them. He had the stronger urge to shove it aside and go for his father's throat but, he thought wryly, with his luck, the desk wouldn't budge and he'd crash into it and break something. He was good at breaking things. Clumsy as an oaf, he'd once heard his father tell his mother after he had managed to break another bone. If he hadn't been aware of his father's disappointment in his only son, he certainly was then.

"I…" The words seemed to catch in his throat as if barbed, and he hated his father even more for making him feel like a boy again in his presence. "I just need to get out of town for a while."

"Where?"

Anywhere. As far away as he could get from Antelope Flats, Montana. "I'd like to go down to Texas. Maybe go back to school." He was grabbing at anything he could think of.

"What is this really about?" Mason VanHorn demanded.

His father always saw through him. Mason VanHorn held the purse strings, so he also had a stranglehold on Holt's life.

"Please just give me enough money to—"

"Is this about Rourke getting out of prison today?" Mason demanded.

Holt heard the disgust in his father's voice, saw the worry in his face. No, not worry, the affirmation of what his father had suspected for years.

"All I need is enough money to tide me over—"

"VanHorns don't run like cowards," his father said through clenched teeth.

"Right." Holt saw then that his father would freeze in hell before he'd help him get away from here. "Never mind. I should have known you wouldn't help me."

He turned too quickly, bumping into the end table. The table overturned. The bronze cowboy hit the tile floor with a crash and a curse from his father.

Holt didn't stop to pick up the bronze or the table. He headed for the door, wondering how far he could go on thirty-seven dollars and fifty-two cents.

"If you run, everyone will know you have something to hide," Mason VanHorn yelled after him.

Chapter Three

Cassidy had never run from anything in her life. But as she stood in the kitchen of the Longhorn Café smelling the freshly baked rolls that had just come out of the oven, every instinct told her to take off. Now.

Rourke was back. She could feel it. The rest of the town seemed to have given up on him. The café had cleared out as the day dragged on and he hadn't shown. Ellie was taking care of what few customers were left. Cassidy had gone into the kitchen to help Arthur, her cook, who was working on the nightly dinner special.

Trying to keep to her usual routine, Cassidy made the dinner rolls for that evening. She liked cooking and baking. Especially making bread. She could work out even the worst mood kneading dough.

But it didn't work today. Nothing worked. And she knew she had to get out of here. Out of the café. Maybe out of town. The state. The country. She couldn't face Rourke. Not today. Maybe not ever.

"I'm going to take off for a while," she told Ellie, who was sitting in an empty booth reading a magazine, waiting for Kit, the night-shift waitress to come in.

"You all right?" Ellie asked.

"Yeah."

"He's not coming back to town. Hell, if I were him I'd head for Mexico or maybe South America," Ellie said. "I've seen pictures of it down there. It's nice." Ellie was always dreaming of going somewhere else. But at almost fifty, it wasn't looking like she would ever go any farther than a couple of hours away to Billings or the thirty-mile drive into Wyoming to Sheridan.

"Everything under control?" Cassidy asked Arthur as she stuck her head in the kitchen.

The cook was forty-something, tall, pencil thin, with a shock of dark hair beneath his chef's hat. He gave her a look filled with sympathy. It was the last thing she needed right now. "Take care of yourself, sweetie."

She smiled and nodded, taking off her apron and hanging it up before heading into the small office at the back. Retrieving her purse, she glanced around to make sure there was nothing she would need.

How could she know what she would need? She had no idea where she was going. Or if she was even going any farther than home. She was new to running and it already didn't suit her.

She turned out the office light and started down the hall toward the back door.

"Not planning to skip town, are you?" asked a strident voice behind her.

Cassidy froze.

"Not Cassidy Miller," the voice mocked.

She turned slowly, a curse on her lips as she met her

cousin's blue-eyed gaze. "I'm going home for the day, not that it's any of your business."

Blaze Logan nodded, smiling as if she'd always been able to see through her.

Cassidy feared that might be true.

"No one would blame you if you turned tail and ran," Blaze said in her comforting, I'm-your-friend tone.

Cassidy had fallen for that act when she was young and stupidly confided in her cousin. She was no longer that young or naive. Normally she avoided Blaze when at all possible and Blaze hadn't gone out of her way, so their paths had crossed little in the past eleven years. Cassidy should have known that Rourke's return would change all of that.

"What would I have to run from?" Cassidy asked as she stepped toward her cousin.

Blaze laughed, a bray of a sound. "Rourke McCall."

"I have nothing to fear from Rourke." If only that were true.

Blaze eyed her. "I just saw his pickup go by."

Cassidy suppressed a shudder, hoping she hid her emotions as well. "Go away, Blaze. This doesn't have anything to do with you. Or does it? I've always suspected you knew something about Forrest's murder, something you don't want Rourke to know."

Blaze paled under the thick layer of makeup she wore. "That's ridiculous."

"Is it?" Cassidy raised a brow. "I wonder if Rourke will think so?"

"Don't you dare try to incriminate me," Blaze snapped. "You start telling Rourke a bunch of lies—"

"Oh, I'm sure Rourke has had a lot of time to think about the past. He's probably figured out by now why you danced with Forrest that night."

"How could I know that Rourke would try to cut in, let alone that Forrest would pick a fight with him?"

"Oh, Blaze, I think you knew exactly what you were doing. Everyone had heard the rumors going around about you and Forrest. And all the time Rourke thought he was the only one you were seeing. It certainly gave Rourke a motive for murder, didn't it?"

All the color had gone out of Blaze's face. "You started those rumors," she said on a whisper. "You would have done anything to break up Rourke and me."

Cassidy let out a laugh that was almost a sob. "It was a junior-high crush, Blaze. I much prefer his brother Cash." Cash had asked her out a few times. She'd declined.

But Cassidy knew Blaze was interested in Cash.

"Cash?" Blaze demanded in a choked cry. "You and Cash?"

"Oh, I'm sorry," Cassidy said. "Are you interested in him, too?" She hated the cattiness in her voice. "You change McCall brothers the way you change shoes. It's hard to keep track. Whatever happened to J.T. McCall? Didn't work out?" J.T., the eldest and the one in charge of the ranch, hadn't given Blaze the time of day. Cassidy had seen him cross the street to avoid Blaze. Cassidy knew that feeling only too well.

Blaze glared, nostrils flared. "Be careful little cousin. If Rourke doesn't kill you just like he did Forrest, someone else might." With that, she spun around and stalked out of the café.

Cassidy stared after her, feeling weak and sick. Blaze always brought out the worst in her. But it was Blaze's last words that struck to her core. What would an embittered Rourke McCall do? Would he make good on his threat to see her pay for her part in sending him to prison?

She wondered now why she hadn't run the moment she heard Rourke was getting out of prison. Her stupid pride. She didn't want the town to think she was a coward. Or that she had anything to hide.

Both were a lie.

She took a breath, then went back into her office, turned on the light, put her purse away. She had work to do. As much as she wished otherwise, she wasn't cut out to be a runner.

ROURKE DROVE all the way through Antelope Flats, surprised at how little it had changed. There were a few new houses on the edge of town, a half-dozen different businesses, but basically in eleven years the town had changed little.

Antelope Flats was like so many other small Montana towns. There were more bars than banks, more churches than places to eat. There was no mall. If you wanted to buy clothes, you either went to the department store on Main that had had the same sign out front since the 1950s or you went to the Western store where you could also buy a rope or a hat or a pair of boots.

What was new was Antelope Development Corporation or ADC as Brandon had called it. Rourke hadn't noticed the office the first time he drove past. He'd been too busy looking across the street at the Longhorn Café.

He'd always asked Brandon about Cassidy, afraid she might clear out of town before he got out of prison. So he knew that Cassidy had bought the Longhorn Café and it had been thriving under her management. She'd also bought the old Kirkhoff place at the edge of town.

"And Blaze?" Rourke would ask his brother.

"She's working for Easton Wells. He started ADC across the street from the Longhorn."

"What's ADC?" he'd questioned, frowning.

"Antelope Development Corporation. Mostly they deal with landowners and coal-bed methane gas well leases."

"Our old man must love all those wells everywhere around the property," Rourke had said. Asa McCall would shoot anyone who even suggested doing anything to his land but farming and ranching it.

"There's money in that gas," Brandon said. "A whole lot of money. You can't believe the wells that have gone in around the county."

"Blaze seeing anyone?"

Brandon would shrug. "You know Blaze."

Yeah. He knew Blaze, he thought as he pulled into a space in front of the Longhorn Café and sat for a moment trying to see inside the café through the front window. The afternoon sun made the glass like a mirror, reflecting him and his old pickup.

He'd been waiting for this day for so long he could hardly believe it had finally come. He got out, slammed the truck door and walked toward the entrance to the café. Town seemed a lot busier than it had eleven years ago.

He saw people he used to know, but he didn't acknowledge them. Most just stared. He knew he'd changed in the past eleven years. He told himself maybe they didn't recognize him. Or maybe they didn't want to. Maybe they were afraid of him.

He pushed open the door to the Longhorn. The bell tinkled and he stepped into the café, and was hit by the mouthwatering smell of freshly baked bread.

His stomach growled and he realized he hadn't eaten since breakfast. He took a stool at the counter. The café was empty this late in the afternoon except for one couple he didn't recognize at a booth. He could hear voices in back, the clang of pots and pans, the creak of an oven door opening and closing.

He picked up a menu, telling himself that Cassidy probably wasn't even here. The menu covers were the same plastic with a local color photograph of red bluffs, tall blue-green sage and a longhorn steer in the foreground. It had been a shot of the McCall Ranch. He liked that she hadn't changed it. And wondered why she hadn't, given how at least one McCall felt about her.

The McCall Ranch was the only one around that raised longhorns. There was no money in anything but beef cattle, but his father kept some longhorns, raising them as his great-grandfather had. A reminder of what had started the ranch, a link to the past that Asa hadn't been able to let go of.

Out of the corner of his eye, he saw Cassidy come out of the back of the café. She didn't recognize him at first. Not until he looked up from the menu and his eyes met hers.

CASSIDY STOPPED dead in her tracks. Although all day she'd been expecting to see him walk into the café, she was shocked to see Rourke sitting at the counter, shocked that after all these years, he really was free and home.

Her heart thudded in her chest so loudly she swore he had to have heard it. Except he wouldn't know why. He'd think it was out of fear.

Her biggest shock was how much Rourke had changed. He'd been more of a boy than a man when he'd left, tall and lanky, not yet filled out at twenty-two.

Now there was no doubt that he'd become a man, from his strong jawline to his broad, muscular shoulders. But there was a coldness to him that showed in the pale blue of his eyes, a hardness that hadn't been there before. Bitterness and anger showed in the hard set of his jaw, in the way he carried himself, a wariness, a spring-coil tension like a wild animal that knew he had predators nearby.

Her heart dropped at the thought. Rourke believed she was one of those predators. She shuddered to think what his life had been like the past eleven years in prison. And the part she'd played in sending him there.

"Rourke," she said, and forced her feet to move toward him, careful to keep the counter between them. She put down the rack of glasses she'd been carrying, shoving her shaking hands deep into her apron pockets so he wouldn't realize how much just seeing him affected her.

She glanced past him to the street and beyond it to the large window of the ADC where Blaze was standing, watching them. Her stomach churned. Blaze was hoping for a show. What *did* Rourke have planned?

"Cassidy." There was a softness to his voice that belied the icy malice in his expression.

His voice was the only thing about this man that was the same as the boy she'd been unable to get out of her thoughts for years. She hated what just the sound of that voice did to her.

"I heard you were released," she said, needing to say something. "I'm glad you're back."

He smiled at that. "I'll bet." He looked down at his menu.

"Rourke, I—"

"I'll have the same thing I used to."

A hot roast beef sandwich, a coffee and a salad with blue-cheese dressing.

She stared at him. "I was hoping—"

"You do remember what I used to order when your mother worked here, don't you?"

Fumbling, she pulled her pen and order pad from her pocket and wrote down his order, writing fast so he wouldn't see how her hands shook.

He smiled a smile that had no chance of reaching his eyes.

There was so much she wanted to say to him, but she could see he wasn't going to let her.

Back when she and Rourke were teens, Cassidy's mom would have taken Rourke's order. Cassidy would have been bussing tables, lurking in the kitchen so Rourke wouldn't see her, feeling ashamed to be caught sweaty, in her white uniform, her apron soiled from clearing dirty tables.

He was looking at her as if he knew her deepest, darkest secrets, knew that she hid in the kitchen when he came in, and listened to him talking and joking with her mother.

"Anything else?" she asked, looking down at the scribbled order on her pad, then up at him.

"No." His expression was colder than the grave.

She stared at him, confused. She'd expected him to lay into her the moment he saw her. She wished he had. His silence was more frightening. Tension arced between them like a tightwire. She felt as if she were balancing on it, unsteady, ready to fall any moment.

"I'll put your order in," she managed to say.

He picked up the menu to look at it again, then without a word turned away from her to stare out the front window, toward ADC and Blaze? He was enjoying her discomfort. He wanted to make her suffer, drag this out.

She turned and walked back to put in his order, trying hard not to run. She wished Kit would come in for her shift, but Cassidy knew she wouldn't leave anyway. She couldn't escape Rourke. Not in a town the size of Antelope Flats. Not even in a state as large as Montana.

Needing desperately to keep busy and yet not wanting to hide in the kitchen, she returned to the counter with more clean glasses and utensils.

She could feel his attention on her, hard as stones, but he didn't say a word. Nor did she try to talk to him. It was clear Rourke was calling the shots.

Kit came in finally, passing Cassidy and making big eyes at her as if to say, *Did you see who's sitting at the counter?*

"You want me to wait on him?" Kit whispered on one of Cassidy's trips to the kitchen.

"No, I have it covered," she said, wondering if Rourke was straining to hear their conversation, just as she had strained to hear his so many years ago.

She returned to the counter to refill the sugar, salt and pepper containers. The one time she looked in his direction he was smirking at her as if he knew what she was up to and it didn't fool him for a minute.

She should have picked another task to do. She spilled sugar, knocked over salt and pepper shakers, fumbled and dropped things. *Come on, Rourke. Just get it over with.*

The bell dinged that his order was up. She hurried back to get it, so nervous she felt nauseous.

She wiped perspiration from her forehead with her arm. Her skin felt flushed, then dimpled with goose bumps as a chill rippled over it. She blotted her hands on a clean towel, avoiding the sympathetic looks of Ellie, Kit and Arthur.

"Don't you want me to call the sheriff?" Arthur said.

"No!" She lowered her voice. "Please. I can handle this."

Picking up Rourke's order, she hurried back out to the counter and put it down in front of him.

"Thank you," he said, his eyes boring into her.

"Can I get you anything else?" Her voice only broke a little but she could see that he heard it, relished in the fact that he had her flustered.

"No thanks. I have everything I need. At least for the moment," he added.

She was weary of this game and desperate to say the words she'd wanted to say to him for eleven years. "Rourke, I think we should—"

"I'll let you know if I need anything else," he said, cutting her off.

He didn't want to hear her tell him how sorry she was for what had happened to him. Or how badly she felt about the part she'd played in it. He wanted to be angry.

To make her suffer. Didn't he know how much she'd suffered already?

No, she thought, looking into all that icy blue. He wanted to strike out at her for his own suffering. He wanted someone to pay. And he'd decided eleven years ago, who that person would be.

She stared at this hardened, cold, embittered man with only one thing on his mind: getting even with her. The realization left her feeling empty inside.

He'd never paid her any mind at all—except for one kiss when she was thirteen and then again after Forrest's murder. He'd looked right through her before then.

She refilled his coffee cup. He thought she'd framed him for murder. That he'd been the only one to live his life under a cloud of suspicion for the past eleven years.

If he thought he could make her feel more guilty, he was wrong. She had blamed herself all these years.

Just do it, Rourke. Do whatever it is you've been planning to do to me for the past eleven years.

He must have seen the change in her. His eyes narrowed and he frowned as if suddenly confused.

There was a crash of pots and pans from the kitchen, followed by some mild cursing. Cassidy hurriedly returned to the kitchen.

Arthur looked up sheepishly. "Nerves," he whispered.

She smiled at him, knowing how he felt, and bent to help him and Kit retrieve the clutter of pans that had fallen from the shelf. Ellie had finally left, it appeared. "These all have to be washed."

"I'll do it," Kit volunteered, kneeling beside her on the floor. "Are you all right?" she whispered.

Cassidy nodded. She felt as if she'd just gotten the news that someone close to her had died. Only she and Rourke had never been close. Their only connection was his need for revenge. And her need to set things right.

She'd tried to just before Rourke was moved to the prison in Deer Lodge. She'd gone to the jail to try to talk to him but he'd been too angry to listen—let alone believe her.

Cassidy handed Arthur a pan as she rose. Hiding her tears, she made a swipe at them, then turned to go back out to the counter. Rourke *would* talk to her. And if he didn't, well, she'd talk to *him*.

But when she reached the counter, she looked around in confusion.

He was gone.

She stared in surprise at the spot where she'd left him just minutes before. His plate was empty. He'd left the price of his meal and a generous tip on the counter.

She was torn between relief and regret. Both made her weak. She leaned against the counter, fighting back her earlier tears. She felt drained, bereft.

"Go on home," Kit said as she scooped up Rourke's empty dishes and wiped down the counter. "You've had a long day."

Cassidy could only nod. It had been the longest day of her life.

She took off her apron, hung it up and went to her office to retrieve her purse again. This time, she didn't hesitate. She opened the back door, trying not to run. She desperately wanted to go home, take a hot bath, mourn for all that had been lost.

The door swung open and she stepped out.

Rourke was leaning against his old pickup, arms folded across his chest, his cowboy hat pushed back, the last of the day's sunlight on the face she'd dreamed about for eleven years. Some of those dreams had turned into nightmares.

Chapter Four

"Let's go for a ride," Rourke said, motioning to his pickup as he considered what he would do when she refused.

Cassidy glanced at the truck, then at him. "If you want to talk, we can go in my office."

"Any reason you wouldn't want to go for a ride with me?" he asked.

She cocked her head at him, that look in her eyes again, the same one he'd seen earlier in the café. Anger? What the hell did *she* have to be angry about? He thought of the photo in his pocket. He didn't know what to make of it any more than he did of her now. He would have to learn to read this woman better.

"I know you're trying to intimidate me," she said quietly.

He smiled at that. He'd just graduated from the school of intimidation. "That's what you think I'm trying to do?"

"Yes," she said, but to his surprise, she walked around the front of the pickup, opened the passenger-side door and climbed in.

He was momentarily taken aback. He'd expected her to put up an argument. Maybe even yell for help. Or at least threaten to tell his brother the sheriff that she was being harassed.

She'd surprised him and he had a feeling it wouldn't be the first time. That in itself worried him as he climbed behind the wheel and glanced over at her.

"You know most people in town wouldn't have agreed to a ride with a convicted killer," he said as he shifted into first, kicking up gravel from the rear tires as he took off.

She just shot him another one of those looks he couldn't read. Everything about Cassidy was a mystery to him, he realized. He'd been four years ahead of her in school. He barely remembered her. Even after high school when she'd gone to work at the Longbranch that summer before college bussing tables, he hardly remembered seeing her.

And even after hiring several private investigators while in prison to dig up everything they could on her, he still didn't have any idea why she'd framed him. Or who was really behind it.

Cassidy Miller appeared to be just what she seemed. A twenty-eight-year-old woman who'd grown up in Antelope Flats without a father. Her mother had been a waitress. The year her mother died, Cassidy was at Montana State University in Bozeman on a scholarship, getting a degree in business.

Cassidy had come back to Antelope Flats, bought the Longhorn Café and later the Kirkhoff Place, both with low down payments.

She was up to her eyeballs in debt but had made a go of the café and had never been late on a payment on either place. She'd never been in trouble with the law.

Never even been late on returning a library book from what he could tell.

On the surface, Cassidy Miller looked squeaky clean. He wondered what he'd missed.

"Where are you taking me?" she asked as he drove out of town headed north. There was only a slight quiver in her voice. She was trying so hard to make him think he didn't frighten her. Fool woman.

"You'll see."

She wore a pale pink short-sleeved uniform top and skirt that came down to her knees.

He remembered her in jeans, boots and a Western shirt. Now that he thought of it, she had dressed like his tomboy sister, all cowgirl. He couldn't ever remember seeing Cassidy's legs before. They were shapely, lightly tanned from the summer and long for her height of about five foot six. She was short next to him at six-two.

With her small leather purse in her lap, white cross-trainers and white socks on her feet and her hair pulled up in a ponytail, she looked like the schoolgirl he'd kissed in the barn. Except, he noticed as he drove, her body had filled out. She'd turned into a woman while he'd been gone, he thought, annoyed with himself for noticing, even more annoyed with her for not being the same person he'd imagined when he'd planned what he would do to her.

He drove north five miles, turned onto the Rosebud Creek Road and didn't go far up the winding muddy path before stopping next to a monument with the word *Crook* on it.

"Come on. Let's take a little walk." He climbed out before she could argue. He could tell she wasn't wild about the idea, but she opened her door and stepped out, squinting into the sun that was about to sink behind the bluffs.

She should have been terrified. And would have been, if she'd known how furious he was with her. He was convinced there was only one reason Cassidy Miller had gotten into the pickup with a convicted murderer. Because she knew he wasn't a killer. Because she knew who was and had kept silent all these years while he was locked up in prison.

He started up a gully through the tall grass, walking toward the bottom of the red bluffs. It was cool here with the sun almost down. The air smelled of sage and pine. A bee buzzed in the riot of wildflowers, and crickets chirped deeper in the bushes.

He'd waited so long for this day he could hardly contain himself. He took deep breaths, fighting to control his temper. He wanted to grab Cassidy and shake the truth from her.

Instead, he looked at the red bluffs, at the ponderosa pines along the top and imagined Cheyenne and Sioux warriors sitting on their horses watching them.

He'd always liked to come here. His grandfather had brought him the first time and told him the story of struggle and courage, victory and defeat, the tale of man's battle against man. He'd felt the history then, just as he did now, as if it was entrenched in the soil, in the rocks.

"Why are we here?" Cassidy asked as he stopped in a draw below the red bluffs. The breeze stirred her hair, now loose around her shoulders. She had pulled out the band that had held her hair and was nervously toying with it.

"Do you know what happened here?" he asked.

She glanced behind them, down the hillside. He followed her focus to where the lush green willows, wild roses and chokecherries hid the stream. They were completely alone. The closest ranch house was a good half mile away and there had been no vehicles at the ranger station up the road when they'd passed.

"Everyone knows what happened here," she said, turning back to look at the bluffs, then at him.

He smiled at that. "I doubt few people have even heard of the Rosebud Battlefield, let alone know the story."

General Crook and his men had stopped to water their horses at the creek on June 17, 1876—just eight days before the Battle of the Little Bighorn. Fifteen hundred Cheyenne and Sioux warriors came over the hills above where he and Cassidy now stood and attacked the cavalry unit.

Of Crook's one thousand men and three hundred and seventy-five Crow and Shoshoni scouts, only eight cavalry men were killed and fifty scouts.

It wasn't much of a battle because Crook didn't pursue when the Indians retreated. But eight days later, the warring warrior chiefs used the techniques they'd learned on the Rosebud to defeat Custer at the Little Bighorn. Custer and two hundred and sixty-one cavalry and scouts were killed.

Cassidy gave him a look that he *could* read. What was the point of all this?

"Crook didn't go after the Cheyenne and Sioux that day," Rourke said. "If he had, who knows how history might have been written. Instead he just let it go not realizing he would contribute to many more deaths at the Little Bighorn."

She shook her head and met his gaze. Her eyes, he noticed, were the same color as her hair, shades of rich brown in the sunset with splashes of gold.

"You're not going to let it go," she said. She didn't sound in the least surprised as she turned her back on him to look down at his pickup parked below them on the hillside. If anything, she sounded sad.

"There are some battles that you just can't walk away from," he said. "But that isn't my point. Crook was in the wrong place at the wrong time. Historians disagree, but I think he made a mistake not finishing the battle and I—"

"I'm sorry." Her voice broke as she turned to face him. "I never meant to hurt you. I tried to explain about that night."

Rourke squeezed his eyes closed, that night too clear in his memory. Driving up the dark gulch, driven by his anger. Forrest's pickup flashed in his headlights. He'd swung his truck in front of Forrest's because he thought Forrest would try to make a run for it. And then he'd stormed over to Forrest's truck and jerked open the driver's side door.

Forrest had fallen toward him and, without thinking, he'd caught him. Blood. It was all over his hands, his shirt, as he'd pushed Forrest back up in a sitting position behind the wheel. Everything registered at once. The gunshot wound to Forrest's chest, the dead, hollow look in his eyes, the empty seat beside him.

He'd stared at Forrest, trying to make sense of it, then turned and ran back toward his pickup. He'd left it running, the lights on. He had to get help. That was what he'd been thinking and yet he'd known Forrest was dead. Did he reach his pickup? Rourke couldn't be sure.

All he remembered was Cash waking him up in the wee hours of the morning. He had Forrest's blood all over him and the murder weapon was on the seat next to him with only his fingerprints on it. And Cassidy. She stood out in the darkness, hugging herself, beside Cash's patrol car.

And Cash was saying, "Cassidy called, worried after you left the Mello Dee." Cassidy, the one who'd tricked him into going up Wild Horse Gulch in the first place.

He fought to keep eleven years of anger and frustration and bitterness out of his voice and failed. "Stop lying to me. You wouldn't have gotten into my pickup today if you thought I really was a murderer. You know I didn't kill Forrest, because you framed me for his murder. I want to know why. And who was in on it with you."

She had to have heard the rage in his voice, seen it in his eyes, in his balled fists at his side. And yet she met his eyes and didn't veer away. "I don't know who killed Forrest. I just know in my heart that you didn't do it. You couldn't kill a man in cold blood, not even out of jealousy." She shook her head. "Why can't you believe me?"

"Because I didn't believe your story at the trial and I sure as hell don't believe it now."

"The prosecutor used me to help convict you. I'm sorry about that. But I told the truth and I give you my word that I'm telling you the truth now. There is nothing more I can do." She started to walk past him back down the hillside to the pickup, but he grabbed her arm and spun her around to face him.

"Not so fast, sugar." He smiled at her. "Your *word?*"

She raised her chin, her spine a rod of steel. "It's all I have."

He felt the fury, banked for so many years, bubble up inside him. "I'm not taking your word on anything, all right? You wrote the note that put me up Wild Horse Gulch, that put me at the scene of the crime."

Her chin came down a little, some of the steel melting out of her spine. "I'm not proud of what I did."

"Not *proud?*" he echoed. "It cost me eleven years of my life. You set me up. The killer couldn't have framed me without you leaving me that damned note!" He was towering over her, his fingers digging into her arm.

"Do you think that I haven't agonized over this every day for the past eleven years? I tried to save you at the trial. You know I did." Tears welled in her eyes but she didn't look away. "You're hurting me." It came out little more than a whisper.

He released her at once, swallowed and stepped back, afraid of what he might do to her. Overhead, a hawk sailed soundlessly across the fading blue sky. "Why did you write that note?"

THE PAIN IN HIS VOICE crushed her heart like a blow. She felt hot with shame just as she had at seventeen when she'd taken the stand to explain that she'd left a note on Rourke's pickup windshield telling him that Blaze was meeting Forrest up Wild Horse Gulch.

That spiteful note, written out of her schoolgirl jealousy over Rourke and Blaze, had cost Rourke eleven years of his life. She'd helped send him to prison, destroying the young man he'd been. All these years she'd hoped that when he got out of prison he might finally believe her. What a fool she'd been. Then. And now.

He stepped back, shoved his hands deep into the pockets of his jacket, as if fighting to control his anger. "Tell me something. What would *you* do if you'd just spent eleven years of your life behind bars for a crime you didn't commit?"

"I would find the real killer or die trying," she said without hesitation.

He smiled at that. "And what would you do once you found him? Or *her,*" he added.

She swallowed, afraid of where he was going with this. "I would prove the person was guilty and turn the evidence over to the authorities."

His laugh held no humor. "Then I guess you and I are different."

"I hope you don't intend to take the law in your own hands," she said, her voice cracking. "It will only get you sent back to prison."

Rourke closed the distance between them in a stride, his hand coming out of his pocket to cup her jaw. He moved so fast she didn't have time to react. But she couldn't help flinching at his touch.

He smiled, obviously pleased to think that he'd frightened her. It had been fear that his touch induced and something much more primitive.

He said between gritted teeth, "If I was going to take the law into my own hands, don't you think I would do it right now?" His thumb caressed her cheek.

She didn't move, didn't breathe.

"I was headed home that night," he said, his voice breaking with emotion. He released her but stayed so close she could smell his masculine scent, feel his heat. "Blaze had already left to go to her apartment. I only went up Wild Horse Gulch because of your note. *You* put me at the murder scene. Don't you dare tell me it was just a coincidence." He glared at her, his eyes a dark blue under the brim of his cowboy hat. "Either *you* framed me. Or you helped someone else frame me and I will get the truth out of you—one way or the other."

She swallowed, her heart breaking at the sight of his raw pain. "What do you want from me, Rourke? I've told you everything I know. I left the note. It was a childish, spiteful thing to do and I've regretted it for eleven years. At the time, I just wanted you to know the truth about Blaze. I thought I was protecting you."

"You did it for my own good," he mocked.

"No, I did it for very selfish reasons. I thought if you knew the truth…" Her eyes came up to meet his.

"What?" He grabbed her arm and shook her gently. "What were you going to say?"

"I was seventeen." Her voice broke. "I was in…love with you."

He stared at her, stepping back as if in shock.

"You really didn't know." She smiled ruefully, seeing the truth in his eyes.

"You and I never said two words to each other. How could you…" He reached into his pocket and shoved a photograph at her. "That's what you call love?"

With trembling fingers, she took the snapshot from him and looked down at the two young women in the snapshot.

"How do you explain your anger at me in that photograph?" he demanded. "That was taken just days before Forrest's murder."

"I thought you were taunting me with Blaze."

"What?"

"You were the one who insisted I stand next to Blaze for the photograph. I thought you knew how I felt about you, that you were enjoying rubbing it in my face, maybe hoping Blaze and I would fight over you," she said, and handed him back the photograph.

He stared at her, frowning. "The photo was Blaze's idea. I had no idea how you felt. You never said anything."

She smiled and nodded. "I thought maybe you liked me because— You probably don't even remember that day in the barn." Her eyes burned with humiliation.

"You framed me for murder because I chose Blaze over you, is that what this has been about?" His words hit her like a whip. "I went to prison because of some schoolgirl crush?"

She brushed at her tears, anger replacing the hurt and humiliation. "You didn't go to prison because of some schoolgirl crush. You could have thrown away the note I left on your pickup, and you would have, if you had trusted Blaze. Or if Blaze was trustworthy."

"Oh yeah? Why *did* I go to prison?"

"Because you left your gun sitting out in your bedroom where anyone could take it," she said. "Even if you hadn't gone up Wild Horse Gulch that night, the killer had your gun with only your prints on it. You had motive. You'd just beat the devil out of Forrest Danvers at the bar because he was seeing your girlfriend."

"He wasn't seeing my girlfriend."

She raised a brow. "Wasn't he?"

Rourke swore. "This isn't about Blaze."

She stared at him. "Obviously you're as blind to the truth as you were eleven years ago." She started past him, but he stopped her with a hand on her arm.

"Admit it, you wanted me sent to prison."

She shook her head in disbelief. "If I wanted you in prison, all I would have to do is call the sheriff and tell him you are threatening me."

With an angry gesture, Rourke pulled his cell phone from his pocket and held it out to her. "Go ahead. Call the sheriff. Get me thrown back into prison. Finish what you started."

She stared at him. "Don't you know I would never do that to you?"

"No. Who else hated me enough to frame me for murder besides you?"

"What makes you so sure it was even about you?" she demanded angrily.

"Because I just spent eleven years in prison," he shot back.

"You're that sure you were the target? What if you're wrong. What if it wasn't about framing you but simply about killing Forrest?"

"That's ridiculous."

"Oh? Haven't you been looking for reasons someone wanted to frame you and all you've come up with so far is me? And my motive was that I was jealous of you and Blaze and I set this whole thing up to get back at *you?* I always knew you were arrogant, but I never thought you were stupid."

He looked at her as if he could kill her.

"What if you were just an easy scapegoat?"

He shook his head. "Don't you think I know what you're doing? You're just trying to get yourself off the hook."

She could see from his expression that he didn't want to believe that he'd lost eleven years just because he'd been a convenient patsy. That, she realized, made it worse for him, but it didn't change what she believed had happened the night Forrest was killed and if Rourke was determined to find out the truth—

"I've had a long time to think about this," she said.

"So have I."

"Just consider this. What if the killer wanted to get rid of Forrest and looked around for someone to take the fall?" She hurried on. "You were the McCall bad boy, you kept a gun on a shelf in your bedroom, you were a hothead, you didn't like Forrest and you were going to like him a lot less when you found out about him and Blaze." She waved off his denial. "You were *perfect.*"

He stared at her, his expression grim, as if she'd just voiced his worst fear. Without a word, he turned and walked on up the trail as if wanting to distance himself from her words, from even the thought that they might be true. His lawyer had to have told him the same thing eleven years ago, but he hadn't wanted to believe it. Still didn't.

Cassidy watched him go, his pain so obvious it made her hurt. Could he hate her any more than he had? She hadn't thought so.

Blindly she turned and started down the hill to the

pickup. A sob caught in her throat at the thought that the old Rourke McCall was gone forever, destroyed by prison and injustice and his own bitterness, and that the stranger on the hillside wouldn't stop until he destroyed them both.

Rourke didn't go after her. He couldn't. He fought back the pain and rage that threatened to overwhelm him. He'd had a death grip on one single-minded resolve. To find the real killer when he got out. It was how he had survived prison.

For eleven years, he'd been convinced Cassidy was part of an elaborate setup to frame him for Forrest's murder. He had planned what he would do when he got out. Starting with the note that had gotten him up Wild Horse Gulch that night. Starting with breaking Cassidy Miller. Forcing the truth out of her.

He swore again. He'd had eleven years to think about nothing else. He knew he wasn't without blame. He'd been stupid and hotheaded. What he wouldn't give for another chance to do things differently.

He shook his head, trying to make sense of it. But he'd been trying to do that for eleven years. Except he hadn't known that Cassidy Miller had been in love with him. Is that what this had all been about? She'd left the note that had sent him to prison because she thought she was in love with him?

Or was she right and he had just been a pawn, his own character flaws used against him?

He faced the bluffs and imagined fifteen hundred warriors swarming over the rise. He knew how General Crook had felt.

He wished his grandfather were still alive. Wished

the two of them were standing here now, although Rourke knew he couldn't have taken his grandfather's disappointment in him.

Not that his grandfather would have believed him capable of murder. Just guilty of letting himself be framed for murder. He'd played right into someone's hands. Whoever had killed Forrest had to have known how he was going to react. To Blaze dancing with Forrest. To the note on his windshield.

Two different instances. Two different women. That's why it had made no sense. For years it had just kept coming down to that damned note left on his pickup windshield that had sent him to the murder scene. It always came back to Cassidy.

Cassidy's scream shattered the silence.

He turned to see her scramble back from the open passenger-side door of the pickup, her eyes fixed on something inside, the scream dying on her lips as she tripped and fell.

He was running, fear knotting his stomach as he tried to imagine what had made her scream like that.

"What's wrong?" he called to her as he came around the front of the pickup. Cassidy had scrambled to her feet and was now backing up, her face bloodless as she pointed toward the pickup in sheer terror.

He heard it. The distinctive rattle. At first he didn't see it. Probably because he'd expected it to be curled under the pickup in the shade.

It wasn't. The huge greenish-colored rattlesnake was coiled on the floorboard of the truck, its ugly head raised, the beady eyes locking on him as it struck.

Chapter Five

Rourke swung the door closed just an instant before the snake could strike him. He heard the rattler hit the inside of the door with a soft thump, then there was silence.

"Did it bite you?" he asked Cassidy, unable to disguise the fear in his voice, his insides tightening at the thought of those fangs in flesh.

She shook her head, brown eyes huge.

"Stay here," he said, and walked across the narrow road to a stand of trees where he found what he needed. A long thick stick. Cassidy was still huddled where he'd left her, hugging herself as if it were a bitter-cold winter afternoon instead of a hot fall one.

On the other side of the pickup, he opened the door slowly. Just as he'd suspected, the snake had moved away from the slammed passenger-side door and was now lying under the driver's side on the floor mat.

The rattler coiled again at the sound of the door opening. Rourke had caught more than his share of snakes as a boy. He'd always been fascinated by them rather than repelled.

This rattler was huge and obviously hadn't liked captivity any more than Rourke had. It was mad and just looking for someone to take it out on.

Stepping to one side of the doorway, he used the thick stick to lift enough of the snake to urge it out. The rattler struck the stick, sinking its fangs into the wood and Rourke took that opportunity to pull the snake from the truck.

The rattler dropped to the ground next to the pickup, releasing the stick, looking for its next victim. Rourke didn't move a hair, keeping the stick ready. He'd met guys like this in prison. The snake seemed to eye him for a long moment, then turned and slithered across the road, disappearing into the deep grass down by the creek.

Rourke took a look around the inside of the pickup just to make sure there weren't any other surprises in there. He found a large burlap bag behind his seat, the kind snake hunters used, and swore under his breath.

He stuffed the empty bag back behind the seat and looked out at Cassidy. She was watching. From a safe distance.

"It's all right now," he said, going around the front of the pickup to where she stood. He could see that she was trembling, her face still white with fear. "The snake's long gone."

She glanced around the ground nervously and rubbed her bare arms as if rubbing down goose bumps.

He'd known a few people who were deathly afraid of snakes. The fear defied reason. His father had told him of a guy who jumped out of his pickup at more than forty miles an hour because some fool had put a dead rattler in his truck as a joke.

Rourke saw that kind of fear on Cassidy's face. "Aren't fond of snakes, huh?"

She shook her head, hugging herself again, as she kept an eye on the ground around her. "What was it doing in the truck?"

That was the sixty-four-million-dollar question, wasn't it? "It must have nested in there while I was gone."

She didn't look as if she believed that. "You're sure there aren't any more?"

He nodded, thinking about when someone would have had the opportunity to put the snake bag behind the seat. Probably while he was in the Longhorn. He hadn't locked the truck. Hell, it was Antelope Flats, Montana. Nobody locked their vehicles or even their houses.

And the snake wasn't some sort of joke.

It was a warning. As clear as any he'd ever had.

"I'll take you back to town," he said as he opened the passenger-side door for her.

She studied the floorboard. Looking relieved to find the space empty, she got in and he closed the door behind her.

He stood for a moment, thinking about the snake, then let out a long breath. Fury bubbled inside him like molten lava. But if he'd learned anything in prison, it was how to control his temper. But right now, if he could get his hands on the person who had put that snake in his truck...

He walked around the pickup and slid behind the wheel, angry with himself for bringing Cassidy out here. What had he hoped to accomplish anyway?

Whatever it was, he felt as if it had backfired. The damned woman had him feeling guilty for scaring her with a snake he didn't even know was in his pickup, guilty for hurting her even though he had no idea how she'd felt about him all those years ago.

No, he thought, what was really bothering him was that she had him doubting himself. He'd been so sure that she'd framed him. So sure that once he was free from prison he'd get the truth out of her.

Maybe he had, he thought glancing over at her. And then again, maybe there was a whole lot more to Cassidy Miller yet to be discovered. He knew one thing. He wasn't through with her. She'd be seeing him again. If she thought otherwise, she was sadly mistaken.

They rode in silence back to Antelope Flats. He couldn't quit thinking about what she'd said. What if he hadn't been framed—just used? The perfect patsy. That was certainly him eleven years ago.

But he wasn't ready to rule out Cassidy Miller and a frame job. Not yet. The woman had a jealous streak and had admitted a foolish crush on him. And if anyone did, he knew just how powerful jealousy could be.

He pulled up behind her car at the rear of the Longhorn and glanced over at her. She turned her head toward him, those big brown eyes swimming in tears. Behind them, something he couldn't put his finger on.

A well of emotions hit him like a sledgehammer. For eleven years all he'd felt was his own pain. That and bitter anger. He stared into her face and was filled with regret for hurting her all those years ago.

Cassidy started to say something but must have changed her mind. She opened the pickup door as if suddenly she wanted to get away from him as much as she had that rattlesnake.

"I didn't mean to hurt you when we were kids," he said, surprising himself as much as her.

She seemed embarrassed as she waved off his apology like a pesky fly. "I told you, I was young and stupid," she said as she slid out.

"We were all young and stupid," he said. "But you're wrong, Cassidy, I do remember the kiss in the barn."

His last words were lost as the pickup door slammed, Cassidy giving no indication that she'd heard him.

CASSIDY COULDN'T QUIT shaking. She rushed to her car, her legs weak as she dropped into the seat, closing the door, closing her eyes for a moment, trying desperately not to cry.

Could this day have been any worse? She thought she heard a soft rattle. Her eyelids flew open and she stared at the floorboard, expecting to see a rattlesnake coiled there just an instant before it sank its teeth into her bare leg.

The floorboard was empty. She glanced over the back of the seat. Also empty.

He'd lied about how the snake had gotten into his pickup. She'd seen his expression when he'd found the burlap bag. Someone had put that snake in the pickup. As what? A threat? A warning?

She shivered at the thought. Who would do such a thing?

She started the engine and was ready to pull away before she glanced in her side mirror and saw that Rourke's pickup was still behind her. He was leaning over the steering wheel, his hat hooding his eyes, watching her. How long would he continue to watch her? To follow her? To suspect her?

She met his gaze in the mirror and felt a chill. Putting the car into gear, she pulled away. She'd expected him to follow her, but when she looked in her rearview mirror, he wasn't there.

Still she couldn't quit trembling. He'd dug up all the old feelings. Pain and humiliation and resentment. But it was the old ache that hurt the most. An ache she'd always believed only Rourke McCall could fill.

She didn't know this man who had come home from prison. She let out a laugh. She hadn't known the other Rourke, the wild cowboy who'd made her heart flutter. Who still made her heart flutter.

Cassidy drove south of town and turned onto a short dirt road bordered on both sides by huge cottonwoods. As she drove down the lane, the fallen leaves floated up around her car, golden in the last of the day's light.

The house was small, an old farmhouse that suited her well. It came with twenty acres, corrals and a small barn for her horse and tack. She loved owning land even if it would take most of her lifetime to pay it off.

As she pulled into the yard and cut the engine, she expected to see Rourke's pickup pull in behind her. She sat for a moment, watching in her rearview mirror. No Rourke. Had he given up? She smiled ruefully to herself. Not a chance.

She didn't realize how tired she was as she climbed out of the car and went into the house. What would he do next? That was the question, wasn't it. Rourke McCall wasn't out of her life yet. She wondered if he would ever be out of her thoughts.

It was that carefree Rourke who inhabited her thoughts. The one who had been so full of life and possibilities. When he smiled, his blue eyes had shone like summer sunlight, and just as warm. But there'd always been that hint of mischief in them, too. You never knew what he was going to do next. He probably didn't, either.

She locked the front door behind her and, dropping her purse on the hall table, headed for her bedroom, anxious to get out of her uniform. The old Rourke. She smiled at the memory. Just being around him had made her feel part of something larger than her own life, something exciting and full of adventure.

But Forrest's murder had taken all that away from him. That Rourke McCall was gone. Injustice and prison had killed him.

She felt his bitterness as keenly as he did. Even if he found Forrest's real killer, it wouldn't bring back the old Rourke McCall or eleven years of his life. How could he ever let go of the demons that consumed him?

As she started to undress, she glanced at the large trunk at the end of her bed. The letters. Her heart caught in her throat. Why hadn't she gotten rid of them? If Rourke found out about them—

She shook her head in disgust at her own foolishness.

In the bathroom, she turned on the water in the tub and poured in some of her favorite bubble bath. As she watched the tub fill, she was consumed with an emptiness born of longing. What a fool she'd been. Still was. The Rourke McCall she'd fallen for was gone. She'd waited eleven years for a ghost.

She looked away from the bubbles blooming in the tub and caught her reflection in the mirror. She looked like a woman, but she knew she was still that same lovesick girl, ever hopeful.

She wouldn't cry. She wouldn't. But even as she thought it, tears began to spill down her cheeks.

"Oh hell," she breathed on a sob, as she shed the last of her clothing and stepped into the tub, sinking into the bubbles and letting all the tears she'd never cried finally free.

ASA MCCALL LOOKED for Rourke's old pickup when he returned to the ranch house just before dinner. He cursed under his breath when he saw it was gone. What had he expected? That maybe his son would stay? Would want to work the ranch his ancestors had fought for?

He knew he wasn't being fair. He'd done nothing to convince Rourke to stay. But Rourke was also without a doubt the most pigheaded of his children. If Rourke's mother Shelby were here she'd say Rourke was just like his father.

Asa scoffed at that. Rourke had always been the wild one and if anyone was to blame for that, it was Shelby. But then he blamed Shelby for most of his problems as well as those of their children.

Tonight he let himself wonder for a moment what their lives would have been like if Shelby had been here all these years and quickly pushed the thought away. He couldn't change the past, and thinking about Shelby only made him hurt.

Except lately, he'd been thinking about her more and more. And thinking about the mistakes he'd made, especially with his son Rourke.

"Are you all right?" his daughter asked as he walked into the house. "You've been gone all day. You look tired." Dusty took her father's arm and steered him to his chair, then went to the bar and made him a cold drink. "I'll bet you haven't eaten all day, either."

"Thank you," he said, taking the drink. He was glad she was talking to him again. He hated it when she gave him the silent treatment. He took a long swallow, pleased when she sat down in a chair across from him.

"You were avoiding Rourke, weren't you," she said. "That's why you were gone all day."

He didn't deny it.

"You know he didn't do it," she said, as if continuing a discussion they'd been having earlier. Except she hadn't been talking to him earlier.

"Rourke couldn't kill anyone."

He looked at his daughter. She was so young, so trusting. Maybe he'd lived too long, seen too much, become too jaded, but he knew that anyone could kill or do even worse—especially if he felt cornered or had become bewitched by a woman. And he feared Rourke had been both. Not only cornered that night up Wild Horse Gulch, but out of his mind because of a woman. The wrong woman. They were the ones who drove you to do something stupid.

"We need to help him," Dusty said.

He didn't want her to get mad at him again. But there was no way he was letting her get involved with this quest her brother was on. Asa had already heard from both J.T. and Cash about Rourke's plans to find Forrest's killer.

"I'll tell you what," he said, measuring his words carefully. "I'll help Rourke if you promise to stay clear of it."

She started to argue.

"That's my only offer," he said. "I can help him in ways you can't."

She pursed her lips, eyes narrowed, not happy with his terms but too smart not to see the value in his deal.

"You will ask him to come back to the ranch?"

He nodded. He'd offer but he knew his pigheaded son wouldn't take him up on it.

WHEN EASTON COULDN'T TAKE Blaze's pacing and complaining any longer, he gathered up his papers and stuffed them into his briefcase. "I'm going to finish this at home."

She turned in obvious surprise from the window where she'd been looking out, waiting for Rourke Mc-Call. "You're going home early?"

"It isn't that early, Blaze. Normally you are long gone by now." He gave her a pitying look. "If Rourke was going to drop by, he would have by now." In truth, it gave him no small amount of satisfaction that Rourke hadn't called or stopped in to see her. He could see it was driving her crazy. Her little scheme wasn't working and Blaze was used to getting her way.

Nor was Easton surprised his old friend hadn't come by to see him, either. He wondered what Rourke thought about him being with Blaze now?

Easton swore under his breath, remembering how badly he'd wanted Blaze when she was with Rourke. Had it been Blaze or Rourke's life he wanted? Undeniably he had often wanted to be Rourke. To come from a big ranching family, to have the money and the power and the prestige that went with being a McCall.

Instead, Easton had gotten Blaze. It was little consolation. But then, Rourke had gotten eleven years in prison. Maybe, for once, Easton had gotten the better deal. But as he looked over at Blaze, he wouldn't have bet good money on it.

He dreaded seeing Rourke, but not as much as he dreaded seeing Blaze with Rourke. She would throw herself at him and Easton didn't need to see that. He'd seen enough of that eleven years ago.

"Good night," he said as he headed for the door.

"I thought we were going to have dinner?" she cried.

"Maybe some other night," he said, without turning to look at her. "I have a lot of work to do tonight and you were of no help today." He closed the door firmly behind him before she could argue.

"Rourke McCall," he said under his breath like a curse as he got into his ADC Suburban and drove out of town. "If she wants Rourke, she can have him. Her little plan to make me jealous isn't going to work. No matter what she does."

But that's what worried him as he turned off onto the road to his house on the edge of the bluffs. How far would Blaze go to get him to propose marriage?

Ahead, he saw his house as he came over a rise in the road, his prized possession. He'd had it built on a bluff overlooking the Tongue River and miles and miles of rich bottomland. It had a unique modern design with a long sloping roofline and lots of wood and stone.

He'd done all right for himself, he thought, as he hit the garage-door opener, parked the Suburban and, taking his briefcase, went inside. Even the furniture was modern, sculpted with clean lines. He liked that. Just as he liked the bank of windows that ran the entire width of the house overlooking the river.

It was an impressive view, the winding band of water reflecting the late-afternoon sun, the verdant green river bottom, the red bluffs on the opposite bank rimmed with dark, silken ponderosa pines.

If the house itself didn't relieve a bad day, the view always did. Except for today. He couldn't get Blaze off his mind.

He'd worked for years to accumulate nice things, to afford the comfortable life he knew he should have been born into. He'd made compromises, done things that were necessary at the time but that he now feared would come back to haunt him. His life was in jeopardy. Blaze knew too much about his business, too much about him and the past.

He'd seen it in her eyes. A quiet speculation as if deciding what to do with the information she'd come across. She'd never said anything, but sometimes he felt as if she had a gun to his head.

With Rourke McCall back in town and Blaze playing games, she had cocked the gun and had her finger on the trigger.

As he put down his briefcase and went to the bar to make himself a drink, he rued the day he'd hired Blaze. Sleeping with her was one thing. Working with her was a whole other ball game.

He'd only hired her as a favor to her father—and because John Logan was his silent business partner. Silent and secret. Not even Blaze knew about the exchange of money or the favors her father had demanded in return.

John thought working for ADC would straighten Blaze out. Right.

Easton had actually thought he could free himself of Blaze once he bought her father's share in the company and he tired of her. Except he hadn't bought out her father's share. Nor had he tired of Blaze even though she had always been a liability. Now, though, she was a loose cannon. Blaze thought she could use Rourke, play him for a fool. Again. All she was going to do was get them both into trouble.

Easton took a sip of his drink and looked out at his view, too anxious to enjoy it.

He knew Blaze would still be at the office, pretending to work late, waiting around for Rourke.

He closed his eyes. He could just imagine Blaze turning all her charms on Rourke. The image made him sick to his stomach. He downed the drink.

There had to be some way to stop her from ruining everything.

Returning to the bar, he poured himself another drink and had a thought, one that shocked him. Would he really consider something so drastic?

Chapter Six

As the light started to fall over Antelope Flats, Rourke knew exactly where he wanted to spend his first night of freedom.

But as he drove down Main Street, he couldn't get Cassidy off his mind. Damn her. She'd taken him in with her sweet, innocent act and, fool that he was, he'd fallen for it. She probably thought he'd bought it. Wouldn't she be surprised when he showed up at her door tomorrow.

He couldn't believe that she'd made him feel guilty for hurting her all those years ago and she was the one who should be feeling guilty. He'd come home to get the truth out of her and she'd turned things around so that he felt he should be making *her* feel better.

Worse, for a while there, she'd had him thinking she might be right. That Forrest's murder *hadn't* been about him. That he was just the scapegoat.

He cursed himself as he pulled up in front of the sheriff's house. Hadn't he promised himself he would never trust another woman again?

Sheriff Cash McCall lived in an old Victorian two blocks from the Sheriff's Department. Antelope Flats was an unincorporated town, which meant the only law was the sheriff of what was also the smallest and most isolated county in Montana.

Cash had purchased the house right after college, right after he got the job as sheriff, the youngest sheriff ever in Montana. He'd bought the house as a wedding present for his fiancée, a girl he'd met and fallen in love with at college. Jasmine Wolfe had been driving down from Bozeman to finally meet the rest of the McCalls but never made it. She'd disappeared, never to be seen again. Most people figured she got cold feet about being a sheriff's wife in a dinky little town like Antelope Flats and made a run for it before it was too late.

Cash had searched for her, but it was as if she'd dropped off the face of the earth. His brother had never gotten over her.

He and Cash had that in common. Falling for the wrong women.

"Rourke," Cash said when he opened the door. He'd obviously been expecting him and just as obviously hadn't been looking forward to it.

"No hard feelings, Cash," Rourke said. "I know you were just doing your job when you arrested me and sent me to prison." He smiled to soften his words.

Cash studied him openly for a few moments. Cash was six-four, big as their father, with the McCall blond hair and blue eyes. He was also solid as a tree stump and just as stubborn. Another trait they shared.

"That's real kindly of you, Rourke."

"You going to ask me in?"

"That depends," Cash said. "You going to give me any trouble?"

He shook his head and raised his palms up in supplication. He was just an inch shorter than his brother and in as good shape. "I've learned my lesson."

Cash shook his head but stepped aside. "You had dinner?"

"Ate over at the Longhorn."

His brother swung around, halfway into the living room. "You aren't even thinking about bothering Cassidy Miller, are you?"

Rourke shook his head.

"Because if you are, I will have you back behind bars before you can blink," Cash said.

"I'm aware of that."

They eyed each other for another few moments, then Cash motioned toward a chair. "You want a drink?"

"I could take a beer if you have one," he said, thinking how protective his brother had sounded about Cassidy. Was something going on there?

Cash disappeared into the kitchen and came back with two bottles of beer.

"I thought I might be able to use the family cabin on the lake," Rourke said, twisting off the top of his beer. He took a long drink. Damn, that tasted good.

His brother looked at him suspiciously.

Rourke had to laugh. "I just need a place to stay and, well, I want to be alone and I don't want to have to watch my back."

"Any reason you would have to watch your back?" Cash asked.

"Damn straight. Whoever killed Forrest Danvers might be getting nervous with me back in town. Maybe start feeling a little guilty."

"Did something happen?" Cash asked, looking worried.

Rourke didn't see any reason to tell him about the snake and add to his worry. "Nothing I can't handle."

Cash was shaking his head. "You're going to cause trouble, aren't you?"

"I just served eleven years for a crime I didn't commit. I'd like to know who set me up, but at the same time, I have no desire to go back to prison."

Cash took a sip of his beer and sighed as he sat down across from him. "I investigated the murder, Rourke, along with the state boys who were sent in because we're kin. They had you dead to rights."

Rourke nodded. "Oh, I know all about the evidence. My gun, my fingerprints on it, Forrest's blood on my shirt, the fact that I was found at the scene, the fight with Forrest earlier at the Mello Dee. I also know I didn't kill him." He held up a hand to still his brother as he continued. "Someone went to a lot of trouble to make sure I took the fall for the murder, though. I can't help but wonder why."

"We went over all this eleven years ago, Rourke."

He nodded. "That's why I'm not going to trouble you with any of it."

"If you think that eases my mind—"

"I'd forgotten how good a cold beer tasted," he said. It did feel good to be home.

"You should go fishing for a few days," Cash suggested.

Rourke did a little fishing of his own. "I hear you're not married yet." Of course that wasn't all he'd heard. He'd heard that Blaze had gone after J.T., then Cash and, in fact, hadn't necessarily given up on Cash.

"Have you seen her yet?" Cash asked.

"Blaze? Not yet."

"I meant Cassidy," Cash said, acting surprised Rourke hadn't known who he was talking about.

Rourke eyed his brother. "Saw Cassidy this afternoon. She waited on me at the café and then we went for a drive together."

Cash lifted a brow.

"It's cool. She's going to help me clear my name." One way or another. But he didn't tell his brother that.

"Dammit, Rourke, leave Cassidy out of this."

"Is there something between you and Cassidy I should know about?" Rourke asked, surprised how upset his brother was getting at just the mention of Cassidy Miller.

"She's a nice woman. I don't want to see her hurt. That's all."

That wasn't all. Not by a long shot. He could see that in the way Cash avoided his gaze. Rourke was surprised that it bothered him.

"You know there is one thing that I could use, though," he said. "The file on Forrest Danvers's murder." Cash started to speak but Rourke cut him off. "A copy would do, big brother. Since I already served my time, what could it hurt?"

Cash groaned as he got up. He walked to a desk off the hall, opened a drawer and took out something. "Have you seen the rest of the family?"

"Yep. I can't believe the way Dusty has grown up," Rourke said, shaking his head. "She was just a kid when I left."

Of the McCalls, J.T. was the oldest at thirty-six, followed by Cash at thirty-five, Rourke at thirty-three and Brandon at thirty. They were all pretty evenly spaced except for the baby, Dusty.

Thirteen years after their mother Shelby died, Asa had gone off one day and came back with a baby. He'd told them that Dusty was orphaned, the child of a friend. He'd adopted her and stuck to his story, but the boys had been old enough to know better.

Dusty was the spitting image of the rest of the McCalls and obviously some love child of Asa's, although they'd never known who Dusty's mother was. They didn't blame the old man for being lonesome. They'd never understood why he hadn't remarried.

"After being married to Shelby, I would never dream of marrying again," he'd said the one time Rourke had broached the subject.

Rourke couldn't even remember what his mother looked like. He'd only been three when she'd died, Brandon just a baby. There were no photos of her in the house. Asa said it was too hard on him having her photo around. But J.T. remembered her and maybe Cash. They'd both kept flowers on her grave all these years.

"You know Dad was hoping you'd come back and ranch," Cash said, turning from the desk.

Rourke gave his brother a give-me-a-break look. "He didn't mention that when I saw him earlier today. Maybe he didn't go through with legally disinheriting me but—"

"Who do you think put up the money for your appeal?" Cash said. "I'd hoped you'd come home a little smarter."

"Prison is such an educational place," Rourke

quipped, trying to hide his surprise. The old man had paid for his appeal? "I thought Brandon and Dusty—"

"Dad paid for all of it. He just didn't want you to know," Cash said. "Stubborn pride. Obviously you inherited it from him."

He handed Rourke a key ring with two keys on it. "That's the key for the cabin. The other one's for the boathouse. Seriously, go fishing. Finding Forrest's killer can wait another few days. After all, you've waited eleven years, right? And I'll see what I can do about getting you a copy of your file."

"Thanks." He really meant it. He took the keys, suddenly exhausted. It had been a long emotional day and a damned surprising one. He knew he needed sleep more than anything else. The very last thing he should do was confront the *other* cowgirl he'd been thinking about for eleven years.

BLAZE WAITED at the office until almost seven o'clock for Rourke. She'd worn her sexiest silk blouse, an expensive suit and her highest heels this morning, the ones that flattered her legs, legs encased in the finest silk hosiery money could buy.

And she knew she smelled and looked divine. She'd seen Easton's reaction every time he looked at her or came near her. It did her heart good that he'd been acting jealous all day. He knew she'd only dressed this way for Rourke and it had been killing him.

Except Rourke hadn't shown. Maybe he didn't know where she worked. Maybe he'd gone by her apartment.

But she knew that wasn't the case. Rourke would know where to find her. He just hadn't.

She considered that he might have gotten over her. After all it had been eleven years.

She quickly rejected the thought.

He had written her a letter right after his trial, asking her to write him and to wait for him. She'd written back that it wouldn't be fair to either of them for her to wait and that writing would only make it more painful, but that he would always have a place in her heart. He hadn't written her again. Nor she him.

She had thought about writing him just before he got out. But she hadn't wanted to give Rourke any ammunition in writing that he could use against her. She might want to make Easton jealous, but she didn't want to blow it entirely with him. He was still her best bet for an easy life.

She just hoped Rourke would be as simple to manipulate. She needed him to give Easton that little push he obviously had to have to ask her finally to marry him. She'd given up on using Cash to make Easton jealous. Cash was still hung up on some rich gal he'd met at college who'd disappeared. Even Blaze Logan couldn't compete with a ghost.

And J.T.... she didn't want to think about him. He'd made it very clear he wasn't looking for a wife unless she was interested in being a ranch wife, which meant she was to cook and clean and play mama not only to any children they would have, but also his little sister— and he hadn't minced words about it. He'd had a bad experience with some city girl who had soured him on city girls—and women with careers outside the home.

Blaze, who had no intention of being a career woman *or* a ranch wife, had informed J.T. that if he wanted her, he'd have to hire a cook, a nanny and a housekeeper, because he wouldn't be marrying one.

He hadn't given her the time of day after that. Not that he'd done the pursuing in the first place. All he cared about were his stupid cattle.

But Rourke…well, Rourke should be flattered and grateful for her attention. Especially after all those years in prison. He'd boost her ego and make Easton delirious with jealousy. Rourke couldn't have gotten out of prison at a better time.

She glanced at her watch. Clearly Rourke wasn't coming by. She swore under her breath. As ridiculous as it was, it seemed she would have to do the pursuing. Turning out the lights and locking up the office, she walked out of the building and headed for her car.

That's when she saw him. He was just getting out of his pickup. He stopped and she saw his expression and realized this wasn't the man she used to keep curled around her little finger. Easton was right. Rourke had changed. It crossed her mind that she might be playing with a fire she could no longer control.

But that had never stopped her before, she thought, smiling as she walked toward him. Anyway, this wasn't about Rourke. This was about Easton and her goal to marry him come hell or high water.

"Rourke," she said in her most seductive tone as she stopped so close to him she could feel his body heat and smell the masculine scent of him. He was dressed in jeans and a shirt, boots and a straw cowboy hat. All looked new.

He was more muscular, his body a man's, no longer a boy's, and there was a hardness in his eyes. She couldn't imagine how he could be any sexier even if he tried. And Rourke never had to try.

"Blaze," he said, and gave her a slow, almost calculated smile.

She'd hoped for a little different reaction and felt disappointed that Rourke hadn't burst into her office earlier, swept her up in his arms, kissed her madly and told her that he'd thought about nothing but her all those years in prison. She'd hoped he would carry her off to ravage her as only Rourke could do.

Easton would have just died and word would have spread all over town faster than a wildfire.

Blaze wasn't merely disappointed, she was miffed at Rourke. There wasn't a soul here to see them together. His timing couldn't have been worse. Where had he been? She'd seen him go into the Longhorn Café earlier in the afternoon. If she hadn't decided to pretend to work late, she might not have seen him at all.

She was miffed enough that she decided she wouldn't go anywhere with him when he asked—especially to bed. Not tonight. It probably wouldn't hurt to play hard to get. Look what it did for Cassidy. Blaze had seen the way Cash McCall was always trying to strike up a conversation with her—and Cassidy not even noticing his interest.

"Working late?" Rourke asked, his tone almost mocking as if he knew she'd waited around for him.

"When did you get back?" she asked, changing the subject.

"Earlier." He leaned against the front of his pickup as if waiting for her to make the first move.

She glanced at her watch. This wasn't going anything like she'd hoped.

"You have someplace you need to be?" he asked. He did have a wonderful voice, deep and sexy. Hell, maybe she would let him take her to bed tonight after all.

"Just home. I have an apartment not far from here." How subtle was that?

"What are you driving?" he asked, looking around. She was driving another ADC Suburban parked next to his pickup.

"I walked to work today." A little white lie but one that might get her a ride home, and once Rourke walked her to her door—

"Nice evening for a walk," he said. "I should let you get going." He pushed himself off the front of the pickup, not even touching her as he started around to the driver's side door.

"Did you stop by for something?" she asked plaintively.

He paused to look back at her. "Just wanted to see you. You're not married."

"No." She licked her lips.

"I hope you didn't wait for me," he said smoothly.

She bristled. "We agreed that was the best thing."

"Did we? Funny, I thought it was your decision." He shook his head. "I guess I forgot."

"I'm glad you're back," she called to him as he started to get into his pickup.

"Are you?" He was smiling over the top of the door, then he ducked inside, closed the door and started the engine.

She stood on the sidewalk and watched him drive off. He hadn't offered to take her home. Hell, he hadn't even touched her. Was he angry that she'd broken it off eleven years ago? Like she was going to wait eleven years for him.

Or was he just plain not interested?

No way. He was interested. He was a man. He was Rourke McCall. He was just ticked at her for not writing him or visiting him while he was in prison. He'd be back. Probably later tonight. She wished she'd given him her address. Then she realized her own foolishness. He'd find her. He always had before.

She glanced at the dark green Suburban just feet away and then down at her high, high heels. No contest. She wasn't walking home. She pulled out the keys and headed for the Suburban.

Rourke would have to be punished for not falling all over himself to be with her. She would give him the cold shoulder for a while before she let him make love to her when he showed up at her door tonight. She'd make him park out front. That way Cassidy would see his truck when she drove to work in the morning. So would Easton.

That made Blaze feel better. It wasn't like Rourke had *rejected* her. He couldn't do that. Not as crazy as he'd been about her before he went to prison.

She was deciding what to wear after her shower as she drove to her apartment a few blocks down Main. It should have been a nicer apartment, but her father was still being a bastard and insisting she make her own way.

Which made marriage to Easton Wells look better all the time. But first she deserved one last wild fling with Rourke McCall.

OUT AT THE SUNDOWN RANCH, Asa woke to darkness and the phone. The clock read 3:11 a.m. Nothing but bad news at this time of the morning. He fumbled for the receiver, already shaking, already scared. Rourke. It was his first thought. He hadn't had a call in the middle of the night since Forrest Danvers was murdered.

Heart hammering, he put the receiver to his ear. "Hello?" His voice sounded scratchy, tight. "Hello?" he said a little louder, and pushed himself up in the bed.

He could hear breathing. Not the heavy breathing of an obscene caller but definitely someone on the line. And there was music in the background. A song he recognized.

"Who is this?" he demanded, suddenly more worried. He listened to the soft breathing, holding his own breath. There was a click, then nothing.

He sat for a long moment holding the phone, trying to understand why his heart was racing. It hadn't been about one of the kids. It had been a wrong number.

He hung up the phone, fell back in the bed. Nothing to worry about. His heart pounded as he stared up at the dark ceiling and felt the world around him start to crumble. The soft breathing, the song in the background. He could almost smell her perfume. Shelby. If he didn't know better, he'd think he just had a call from a dead woman.

Chapter Seven

Early the next morning, Rourke heard a vehicle coming up the road to the cabin. One of the reasons he'd chosen this place to stay was because he could hear and see anyone coming. No surprises. He went to the back porch and watched Cash's patrol car wind its way up the mountainside.

The other reason he'd wanted to stay here was the solitude, the beauty, the stark difference between this country and a prison cell.

Having spent too many nights locked up, he'd slept under the stars last night in a bedroll on the beach in front of the cabin. The moon had been almost full. He'd watched it rise over the lake in a kind of breathless awe, feeling the night breeze against his face, feeling alive for the first time in more years than he could remember.

But it had proved to be a restless night, haunted with memories. He'd dreamed about Blaze. And worse, Cassidy. He regretted not taking Blaze up on her offer. He wouldn't make that mistake again.

"Morning," Rourke called in greeting to his brother

as Cash climbed out of the patrol car. "Tell me you brought doughnuts."

Cash smiled as he pulled a large box out with him and headed up the steps. "You realize that's a cliché, cops and doughnuts." He handed Rourke the box.

"Right." Rourke could smell the doughnuts in the bag perched on top of the stacks of papers in the heavy box. "Chocolate covered with sprinkles?" He let out an oath as Cash nodded. "I could kiss you."

"Don't," Cash warned as he pushed open the door for Rourke and followed him inside.

"I made coffee," Rourke said. "You have time for a cup?"

Cash shook his head. "There's a copy of the case file in the box, along with copies of the trial transcript."

Rourke shot him a look. There was no way Cash could have gotten his hands on a copy between last night and this morning. That meant he'd had it all along, had searched, as Rourke planned to, for the real killer.

"Listen," Cash was saying, "I've been doing some thinking."

Rourke put down the box on the table and turned to his brother. Cash and J.T. had always been the serious ones, the McCalls who worried and stewed, the responsible, sensible ones. "If you're going to tell me not to look into the murder—"

"No, that would be a waste of my breath," Cash said with a rueful smile. "Just…just be careful."

Rourke stared at his brother. "You think the killer is still around, don't you."

"I just know there were a lot of hard feelings over Forrest's death and some of what came out at the trial,"

Cash said. "Digging that all up again could be dangerous. You remember how Forrest's brother was? Well,
Cecil's crazier now."

Rourke smiled. "Why can't you admit you don't believe I killed Forrest?"

"Because I'm a cop and I go by evidence, Rourke.
Bring me some evidence to the contrary," Cash said, and
turned to leave. "Enjoy the doughnuts."

And Rourke was the bad boy McCall.

After Cash left, Rourke ate the doughnuts as he considered the huge box full of paper. The doughnuts took
him back to a time when he and his brothers would
roughhouse in the mornings, having pillow fights and
squirt-gun battles, which Martha, the ranch's longtime
housekeeper, would break up with the promise of chocolate doughnuts.

He cherished the memory as he finished the last crumb,
the smell, the taste, taking him back to his boyhood.

Finally he looked in the box on the table. It contained
the reasons he'd gone to prison. Was it possible it also
contained some missed fact that would clear his name
and free him from the past? He knew the chances
weren't good or Cash would have already found it.

For the better part of the day, Rourke went through
every scrap of paper in the box. Head aching, he realized as he turned over the last sheet that he'd exhausted
the possibility of finding a missed clue.

No wonder no one had believed his innocence.

He put everything back into the box and stared at it.
The plan came out of nowhere and yet he knew it had
probably been percolating for eleven years. He grabbed
his jacket and headed for the door.

CASSIDY WENT INTO work as if it was just another day. Her eyes were puffy from crying and she felt horrible, but she put on a little makeup to try to cover it, and a smile. While she probably didn't fool anyone, she was glad she'd come in to work.

The café was packed, obviously with some who were hoping Rourke McCall was going to come in and threaten her again, only this time with a shotgun. What they didn't know was that Rourke's hold on her didn't require a gun.

Rourke didn't show up at all.

But Blaze did. Good old Blaze. She came in and sat at the counter.

"What can I get you?" Cassidy asked, dropping a menu in front of her cousin.

"Just coffee," Blaze said, eyeing her intently. "Are you wearing *makeup?*"

Cassidy didn't reply as she put a cup of black coffee in front of Blaze and left.

Blaze didn't even finish her coffee, Cassidy noticed when she came back by and found her cousin gone. Nor did Blaze leave a tip. Predictable.

As she glanced out the window, she saw Rourke pull up in front of the Antelope Development Corporation and get out. Jealousy raised its ugly head, making her sick to her stomach. This was how she used to feel when she'd see Rourke with Blaze. She turned away as he entered ADC, the door closing behind him. She wouldn't go through this again.

"Is everything all right?" Ellie asked.

"Fine," Cassidy lied.

The bell dinged over the door and she looked up to

see the owner of the Mello Dee Lounge and Supper Club come through the door. Les Thurman brushed a lock of gray hair back from his forehead and headed straight for the counter and her.

"Good morning," he said cheerfully. "Place is busy this morning."

"Good morning." Cassidy could feel him seeing through the makeup and her own cheerful greeting.

"You all right?" he asked. He had a fatherly way about him and had always been kind to her, especially when it came to anything to do with Rourke McCall. Everyone in town must have known how she felt about Rourke—except Rourke. Les had been behind the bar that night at the Mello Dee and no doubt overheard the guys at the bar giving her a hard time about Rourke before the fight broke out.

Now Les glanced toward the front window and Rourke's pickup parked in front of Blaze's office. "If you're dead set on a McCall, consider Cash. He's good and solid. He could make you happy."

She felt herself blush. "The only thing I'm dead set on is getting you some breakfast."

"Sorry. None of my business. I'll take the special," Les said, and picked up a copy of the newspaper lying on the counter. "Keep your nose out of other people's business, Thurman," he mumbled loud enough for her to hear.

She laughed as she hurried off to put in his order.

BLAZE LOOKED UP from behind her desk, unable to hide her surprise at finding Rourke McCall standing in her office doorway. She glanced to the street in time to see

Easton drive away. Had Rourke purposely waited until Easton left the office, until he was sure she was alone? Blaze would bet money on it, she thought as she waited for Rourke to make his move.

"What exactly does Antelope Development Corporation develop?" he asked, coming into the office and closing the door.

She leaned back in her chair and watched him walk around the office. He picked up several pieces of paper from the edge of Easton's desk, glanced at them, then dropped them.

Although his movements didn't seem threatening, she felt a sudden stab of concern. The receptionist must not be at her desk. Otherwise, she would have announced Rourke. That meant Blaze was alone with him and no one knew he was here. Including Easton.

She realized Rourke was waiting for an answer. She smiled, trying to hide the fact that she felt suddenly uneasy. Any sign of weakness could be seen as guilt, she reminded herself.

"Land development."

"Coal-bed methane gas leases," he countered.

She nodded, hearing the distaste in his voice. "Antelope Flats is growing," she said, sounding too perky, as if trying too hard. She could see that he'd noticed. "Methane gas is the future of this town."

"That's too bad," he said.

She smiled up at him as if to make it clear that she didn't care about all this business stuff. She'd worn a robin-egg-blue dress that clung to her curves today.

Easton's eyes had practically popped out of his head when he saw her. She'd flirted with him a little, just to make him feel better.

But it had been hard to hide her delight when he told her he had to go into Sheridan to meet with some coal-mining executives. She could tell he hated to leave her alone in the office. Too bad he hadn't seen Rourke come in.

"So what brings you out this early in the morning?" she asked. She hadn't been sure she would see him again after the way he'd acted yesterday evening. He hadn't called her apartment later last night. Nor had he stopped by. She'd started doubting her control over him. She should have known he couldn't stay away from her.

But what bothered her was the feeling that he hadn't come here to try to get her into bed. And that wasn't like the Rourke McCall she'd known. She feared she didn't know this one at all and that could be her downfall.

How would she know what was going on with him and Cassidy? With him and Forrest's murder? The more she thought about it, the more worried she was that Easton was somehow involved. He'd been acting… scared, and that wasn't like him. What else could it be but Rourke getting out of prison?

That's why she needed to be on the inside of things with Rourke, and there was only one way to get there. Was he going to make her seduce him? Just as she'd done when she was fifteen?

She had more experience now, she thought, and there was no doubt that he'd noticed the dress. But it worried her, Cassidy wearing makeup. Everyone knew what it meant when a woman started wearing makeup. She was after some man.

"I need your help," Rourke said, surprising her by settling down in the chair on the other side of her desk.

Her help? Now they were getting somewhere. She turned up the wattage on her smile. "Just name it."

Rourke would have had to have been dead not to hear the offer in her tone. Blaze definitely assumed they would take up where they'd left off eleven years ago. He'd always enjoyed Blaze. What man wouldn't? Especially when she turned on the seduction, and right now she had it cranked all the way up.

The blue dress hid nothing, making it clear that Blaze's body had only improved with age.

"I'm going to reconstruct the night Forrest was murdered," he told her.

She blinked. It obviously wasn't what she'd hoped for. He almost laughed at her strained expression.

"What?"

"I'm going to reenact that night."

All the color went out of her face. "You aren't serious."

He nodded and leaned back in the chair, meeting her gaze. "All the main players will be there, except Forrest, of course."

"That's the craziest thing I've ever—Rourke, why relive that awful night? I mean it's been eleven years. It isn't like you can uncover any evidence that might have been overlooked."

He shrugged. "You never know."

She took a breath and let it out slowly, making him think Blaze might have reasons of her own for not wanting to return to that night. Hadn't Cassidy insinuated that Blaze might be hiding something?

It irritated him that Cassidy had him second-guessing himself again. Blaze had nothing to gain by setting him up for murder. Did she?

He pushed himself up out of the chair. "So I'll see you at the Mello Dee Saturday night. Come by a little before midnight." He saw Blaze struggling to come up with a good reason she couldn't be there as he started to leave. "Oh yeah, and wear what you wore that night."

"What? You think I still have the same clothes I did eleven years ago?"

He turned to smile at her. "Then just wear something like that outfit you had on that night," he suggested.

"Those clothes have gone completely out of style."

He laughed. "I've missed you, Blaze."

She seemed to like that. "I can't believe *Cassidy* has agreed to this."

"It was her idea," he ad-libbed, and noticed the change in Blaze. She wasn't happy to hear this.

"Cassidy? Rourke, you aren't taking *her* advice, are you?" Blaze let out a pitying laugh. "My cousin would do anything to hurt me. You realize she only got you sent to prison to separate the two of us, don't you?"

He stared at Blaze, realizing just how blind he'd been when it came to her. Cassidy was right. He'd been a patsy and maybe in more ways than one.

"Cash has agreed to stand in for Forrest Saturday night," he said, anticipating Blaze's reaction and relishing in it.

"Cash?"

"Is that a problem?" Rourke asked innocently.

"No, it's just that…" She licked her lipsticked lips. "I suppose you heard about me and Cash?"

He smiled. "If I listened to rumors, Blaze, I'd think you'd slept with every eligible male in town." With that, he turned and walked out the door, closing it firmly behind him.

BLAZE SAT STARING after him, then picked up the first thing she could grab off her desk and hurled it across the room. The stapler hit the wall and clattered to the floor, leaving a gouge in the paneling.

"Bastard," she swore as she watched Rourke walk past his old pickup and cross the street, headed for the Longhorn Café—and Cassidy.

He hadn't even suggested that the two of them get together later, that they take up where they'd left off. Damn him. Worse, he was going over to see Cassidy.

Blaze couldn't believe this. Rourke should have been falling all over her.

She had to do something. Something drastic.

Easton drove up just then, got out of the Suburban, glared at Rourke's old pickup and then headed into the office. Wasn't he supposed to be at a meeting with coal-mining executives? Or had he just told her that's where he was going so he could double back and catch her with Rourke?

Only he hadn't caught her with Rourke. Easton had just missed him. Damn. She scrambled to come up with a way to salvage something from Rourke's visit. Easton had been in a foul mood earlier, had canceled their date last night, and seeing Rourke's truck outside didn't seem to improve his disposition.

She told herself she was getting to him. But she had to up the stakes.

She would pretend she'd left Rourke in her bed this morning and he'd stopped by to…to give her her apartment keys, she thought, hurriedly digging them out of her purse and dropping them on the edge of her desk.

Let Easton think she'd spent the night with Rourke. What the hell. Easton wouldn't know the difference.

She pulled out the small makeup bag she kept in her desk drawer and opened her compact. The look in her eyes startled her. She looked scared and upset. That wouldn't do at all. Not if she hoped to convince Easton that everything was great between her and Rourke, the bastard. They were all bastards.

She heard Easton come in and stop at the receptionist's desk to pick up his phone messages. He would be coming into the office any moment.

Hurriedly she powdered her nose. Pretend you spent a heavenly night in Rourke's arms, she ordered herself. Her gaze softened a little at just the thought.

The door to the office opened and, still powdering her nose, she looked up at Easton and wondered how he was going to take the news about Rourke's plan. Not well, she thought, and realized she was scared, too.

"I'M GOING WITH YOU," Dusty said, her tone brooking no argument.

Asa looked up at his daughter as she came down the wide staircase toward the door where he stood. She looked so much like her mother that for a moment he was dumbstruck by her understated beauty—and her mule-headed determination.

"You're going to town to talk to Rourke, aren't you." she said. "As you *promised*."

"And pick up a load of grain," he said, his real reason for going into town. "Wouldn't you rather stay here? J.T. was talking about riding up into the Bighorns today on horseback."

She smiled and shook her head as if he couldn't fool her. She was *so* much like her mother. "You can buy me lunch in town. Cash told me that Rourke is staying at the lake cabin."

Asa nodded, not surprised by either the news that Rourke was staying at the cabin or that Dusty had wheedled the information out of Cash. "So what makes you think we can even find your brother?"

"It's a small town," she said, and headed for the door.

Asa could see that there was no getting out of this. The alternative was having her go back to refusing to talk to him, which in retrospect might not be so bad.

He followed her out to the truck, not surprised when she started to get in the driver's side. He was touched that Dusty tried to protect him, especially since his heart attack, but he was still the head of this family, dammit.

"I'll drive," he said, stepping past her. He could see she wanted to put up an argument, but he slid in behind the wheel and slammed the door before she could.

She chattered on the way into town about ranch business, the latest news about neighbors and old friends, the upcoming rodeo. He only half listened. He had other things on his mind. Like the phone call last night. He'd convinced himself that it had been a wrong number. Hell, he'd been half-asleep. It wasn't anything to worry about. Nothing at all.

"ROURKE JUST STOPPED BY to drop off my apartment keys," Blaze said, the moment Easton walked into the office. "You aren't going to believe what he's planning to do Saturday night."

"Nice to see you too, Blaze," Easton said, closing the door firmly behind him. He'd gotten little sleep last night, tossing and turning, the night filled with horrible nightmares. He'd awakened in a cold sweat. And now he didn't give a damn what Rourke was planning for Saturday night. In fact, he didn't want to hear the man's name.

"He's restaging the murder."

Easton turned to look at her, her words chilling him to the bone. The woman was powdering her nose. Primping. And he didn't need to wonder for whom.

"What the hell did you do to cause this?" he demanded. Her cheeks were flushed and it wasn't from blush. She was enjoying this, he thought, wanting to strangle her.

"I didn't do anything," she protested. "He just came into the office this morning to give me my keys and announced that he wanted all of us to be at the Mello Dee Saturday night and, get this, to wear the same clothing—as if we still had it. What, we donated it to the museum for safekeeping? Can you imagine? Obviously time stood still for Rourke, but for the rest of us—"

"Blaze, forget about the damned clothes." He couldn't believe this. She was so worked up she was babbling and didn't even realize the consequences of her actions. "Don't you know how dangerous this is?"

She quieted for a moment to stare at him. "Dangerous?"

"Are you a complete ninny?" he snapped. "If Rourke isn't the killer, then who is? Someone we know?"

"That's crazy."

"Your cousin has said from the beginning that someone must have seen her put that note on Rourke's windshield and read it and saw a chance to set up McCall," Easton said in exasperation. "How else did the killer know that Rourke was going up Wild Horse Gulch, how else could the killer have framed Rourke for the murder?"

She was staring at him. "Assuming he *was* framed."

Easton stared back at her. She didn't really think Rourke was a killer, did she? Would she try to use a killer to make him jealous? Was she that stupid?

"Cassidy probably lied," she said.

He shook his head. "Let's not go there again." She'd been singing that song for eleven years, only no one had believed that Cassidy was behind the frame—or the killing. No one except Blaze and maybe Rourke.

"But if Rourke killed Forrest—"

Easton let out a curse. "If you believe that, then how in the hell can you agree to this reenactment? Hasn't it dawned on you that Rourke might be planning this merely to get even with us?"

"Us?" she echoed, her gaze honing in on him like radar. "What are you talking about?"

"This town, Blaze. We sent him to prison. Maybe for a crime he didn't commit. Either way, he's back and clearly he wants to even some score." He shook his head at her.

"If you're worried that Rourke will come after you because you're with me now…"

Easton gave a withering look. "He has already come after me. I found out today that he hired a private investigator who's been snooping around ADC, and I'm not the only one Rourke's been investigating."

"So what?" she demanded with obvious irritation. No doubt she was disappointed he hadn't made something of Rourke returning her apartment keys. She didn't have a clue.

He sighed. "So Rourke isn't going to rest until he gets vengeance. Rourke's going to take down as many of us as he can in that quest." He raised a brow. "Maybe you included, Blaze. I've never believed you went straight home that night and I would wager Rourke doesn't, either."

Chapter Eight

Cassidy hated the bubble of euphoria she felt as Rourke walked into the café. She hadn't expected to see him, just assumed he would be spending the day—if he hadn't already spent the night—with Blaze.

He took a booth in her section rather than sit at the counter, meeting her surprised expression with a smile. He looked different today. More rested, less anxious, she thought as she grabbed a menu, a cup and a pot of coffee and headed toward the booth.

"Hi," he said. "I was hoping you could join me. If you're not too busy."

The afternoon coffee-break crowd had thinned out and it was still too early for supper. She couldn't really decline, even if she'd wanted to.

"Okay." Even with the obvious change in him, she couldn't help but be leery.

"Have you had lunch?"

She shook her head.

"Good. I hate eating alone."

She'd forgotten what his smile could do to her. "You know what you want?" He hadn't opened the menu.

"Chicken-fried steak, biscuits and gravy and whatever comes with it."

She couldn't help but smile as she wrote down the order. When she looked up, he was staring out the window.

"Is that all?" she asked.

He didn't respond and she followed his gaze to see Blaze pulling out in one of the ADC Suburbans. Cassidy had seen her earlier in a blue dress that left nothing to the imagination. Was it any wonder she attracted men like flies to honey?

Cassidy looked away to wipe at a spot on the table with the corner of her apron. She was determined to fight these feelings she had for Rourke. And she refused to be jealous of Blaze. If Rourke wanted Blaze, well, then that was just fine with her.

She hadn't realized he'd turned his attention back to her until she glanced up and saw that he was watching her and seemed to have been for some time.

"I should warn you," he said, as if he knew what she'd been thinking. "I had a talk with Blaze this morning."

"I don't need to—"

"I'm going to reenact the night Forrest was murdered Saturday at the Mello Dee Lounge and Supper Club."

She was speechless.

A sheepish grin moved across his face. "I told Blaze it was your idea."

She gasped. "Why would you do such a thing?"

He smiled and shrugged. "She was so damned sure that you wouldn't go along with it. I couldn't help myself."

"Blaze must be beside herself," she said, and glanced out as her cousin drove away. She caught Blaze's expression. The woman had fury in her eyes as she glared at Cassidy. "I'll put our orders in," she said, suddenly ravenous herself as the Suburban disappeared down the street.

When she returned to the booth, Rourke said, "Beautiful day, isn't it."

Cassidy stared at him, wondering what had changed since yesterday. When he looked at her she'd didn't see the hard anger in his eyes or the brittle bitterness. Instead, she saw something that scared her even more. Hope.

She couldn't bear to see him hurt again and she feared he was setting himself up for a fall by staging the murder night. Worse, by crossing Blaze.

"Rourke, I have to warn you. Blaze can be a little mean-spirited when she doesn't get her way."

He threw back his head and laughed. "She's hell on wheels, but don't worry, I won't let her harm you."

"Me? I was thinking of you."

He shook his head. "You and your cousin couldn't be more different, you know that?"

She knew that. Eleven years ago she would have given anything for whatever it was about Blaze that had made Rourke want her.

"Seriously, are you sure this reenactment is a good idea?" she asked.

He was smiling. "It's a terrible idea. I hope we don't have to go through with it." He met her surprised gaze. "By Saturday, I'm banking on you and me having already found Forrest's killer."

"You and me?"

Was he serious? "Rourke—"

"You made me realize yesterday that I hadn't been paying a lot of attention to what was going on around me eleven years ago."

She felt herself blush and was grateful when she heard the bell announcing that their orders were up. She returned with his chicken-fried steak and a chicken sandwich for herself.

"Thanks," he said, and dug in. "This is great. So, will you help me?" he asked between bites.

Was he really offering her a chance to help him? To redeem herself for the part she'd played in his going to prison? She studied his handsome face. Or was he setting her up, still convinced she had something to hide?

It didn't matter. She would give anything to help him find even a little peace. She couldn't give him back the eleven years. But maybe she could put some of Rourke's ghosts to rest. And some of her own, as well.

"I'll do anything I can to help you," she said. "But, Rourke, I don't know anything. I can't imagine what help I would be."

"You've already helped," he said, and grinned. "By coming up with the reenactment plan." His expression warmed her to her toes.

They ate in silence for a few minutes.

"You've done a remarkable job with this place," he said, glancing around the café, his eyes coming back to her.

"Thank you." She felt shy under the intensity of his attention. This change in him reminded her of the old Rourke, but it also worried her.

"Last night, I thought a lot about what you said," Rourke remarked between bites. "If I really wasn't the intended victim, then that could change our entire approach to finding the killer."

"You're really serious about this, aren't you?" she asked. "I mean finding the killer. I thought after someone put that snake in your pickup yesterday…"

He smiled, his eyes dark. "Only a coward puts a rattler in a man's pickup to scare him. Or a fool. The person who killed Forrest doesn't want to kill again. That's why he's trying to warn me off."

She nodded, not so sure about that.

"I was thinking about your theory," he said as they finished eating.

"That's all it is, you realize," she said quickly.

He nodded. "The thing is, how did the killer know you were going to write the note or that I was going to get into a fight with Forrest that night?"

She'd thought about this for years. "Well, the way I figure it, once he had the gun, all he had to do was wait for an opportunity to present itself—if his true intention was to get rid of Forrest and put the blame on you."

"My gun," Rourke said, and swore under his breath.

"You kept a gun on a shelf in your bedroom," she said, and hated her accusing tone.

"I know what you're going to say."

"Do you?"

"The gun was a…keepsake. I hadn't fired it since I was a boy and my grandfather used to take me out…." He shook his head. "Never mind. The point is anyone could have taken it the night of my birthday party."

She rolled her eyes. "What about in the weeks before the party? The truth is, you don't have any idea when it was taken—or by whom."

"Just for the sake of argument, let's forget about Blaze."

She raised a brow. "Is that wise?"

"I'm not having any trouble with it," he said, meeting her gaze.

"I don't care about your relationship with Blaze," she said, telling herself it was true. "I just think it is foolish to overlook a suspect out of..." She waved a hand through the air as if unable to find the words.

He grinned at her. "Because I'm so besotted with Blaze that I can't think rationally?"

"Yes."

He laughed. "Let me worry about Blaze. I might surprise you." He sobered. "As you were saying, my fight with Forrest that night gave the killer the opportunity he was looking for."

She nodded. "All he had to do was get Forrest to some deserted spot and use your gun with your fingerprints on it."

His eyes narrowed as if he was wondering how her note to him played into her theory.

"Or," she continued, "the killer might have heard the same thing I did—Forrest on the phone setting up the meeting with Blaze."

"You're convinced it was Blaze, even though she denied it in court?"

Cassidy ticked off the reasons on her fingers. "Blaze left early. When was the last time she did that? Never. She used the fight, which she instigated, as her excuse not to see you later that night, right?" She nodded when he saw from his expression that she was right.

"Blaze liked to play hard to get sometimes," he said.

Cassidy wasn't about to touch that. "Also when I saw Blaze and Forrest together a week before the murder, I heard him call her honey bun—just like he called who-ever he told to meet him up Wild Horse Gulch the night of the murder."

Rourke's jaw muscle jumped. "Maybe he called all women honey bun. The guy wasn't very imaginative."

She gave him a pitying look. "Didn't it strike you as odd that Forrest stayed at the Mello Dee after the fight? After the beating you gave him, wouldn't he want to get the heck out of there? So he finishes his drink, glances at his watch, then goes to the phone as if he was wait-ing to call someone. Waiting for her to get home?"

Rourke was frowning.

"He calls a woman—we do agree on that, right?"

Rourke nodded.

"He says meet me and let's talk about it. What would you conclude from that?"

"Okay," he agreed. "I can see how you came to the conclusion you did."

"On top of that, Blaze has no alibi for the time of the murder."

"She lived alone in an apartment. That's not un-usual," he said.

She wanted to slug him and he must have seen the fire in her eyes because he raised both hands in surren-der and said, "Let's say you're right. So where does your note fit into this?"

Yes, her note. "If the killer didn't overhear Forrest on the phone like I did, then he or she had to either see me put the note on your truck or notice it under the windshield wiper—and read it," she said. "But if I hadn't written the note, the killer would have come up with some other way to get you to Wild Horse Gulch— or at least make sure you didn't have an alibi."

Rourke nodded slowly, but she couldn't tell if he agreed with her or was just going along with her theory for the moment.

She didn't point out that Blaze had purposely not given him an alibi by going home alone. "Remember, he already had your gun with your fingerprints on it and you had motive after the bar fight," she said. "I went back inside to the rest room, so I don't know what happened between the time I put the note under your pickup windshield wiper and came back out."

"Why did you go back inside?" he asked.

She looked out the window toward the street and saw that Blaze had returned from wherever she'd been. Cassidy watched her look at Rourke's pickup then glance across Main Street in the direction of the café. There was a glare on the window so Cassidy was pretty sure Blaze couldn't see them. Hoped that were true. There was something in Blaze's expression that chilled her.

"I was upset," Cassidy said, turning her attention back to him. "I'd been crying and I realized that I'd left my purse in the bathroom."

"Maybe you stuck around because you wanted to see what I did when I found the note," he said without rancor.

She dropped her eyes. "Maybe."

He said nothing for a moment. "Did you notice anyone in the parking lot when you went out—other than me?"

She shook her head. "I was too upset…." Her gaze came up to meet his. "Forrest's killer could have been waiting in the parking lot for him and saw me leave the note and read it. Or he could have followed him."

Rourke was shaking his head. "It would have been impossible for anyone to follow Forrest up that road in a vehicle without him knowing it. From where he was parked, he could have seen the car coming."

She nodded and saw the change in Rourke's expression.

"No wonder the jury was so convinced I killed him. So I guess we start with who was there that night. Who witnessed the fight. Who had been waiting for just this opportunity." He shook his head. "You and I, we really played right into the killer's hands, didn't we."

THE BELL OVER THE DOOR JANGLED and Rourke looked up to see his little brother coming in the café. Brandon was scowling. He looked as if he'd slept in his clothing—but not nearly long enough. He needed a shave and he was wearing the same clothing he'd had on yesterday when he'd picked Rourke up in Deer Lodge at the prison.

Rourke knew the look a little too well. At least he had eleven years ago.

Brandon caught his eye and motioned that he needed to talk to him.

"If you will excuse me," Rourke said to Cassidy who had seen Brandon as well. "I need to talk to my brother." He reached into his wallet to pay his bill.

"Lunch is on me," she said.

"Thanks, but at least let me tip the waitress." He

dropped more than enough for both their meals and a tip on the table. "No arguments," he said when she started to protest. Then he hesitated. "Thanks for helping me with this. Can we talk later?"

She nodded.

He stared down into her face for a long moment. He really did like her face. Then he touched her arm, squeezing it as he passed.

"You look like something the cat's dragged in," Rourke said as he let Brandon lead him outside. "What's up?"

Brandon smelled of alcohol and looked even worse up close. "I hate to ask you seeing as how you just got back to town—"

"You need money," Rourke said, and pulled his brother aside. Several people walked by. Rourke waited until they were out of earshot. "I thought you had a job, and what about the money Grandpa left you?"

"I'm in between jobs right now and Dad has my trust et up where I only get a stipend every month," Brandon said angrily. "I can't touch the bulk of it until I'm thirty-five." Five more years.

"How much do you need?" Rourke asked.

Brandon looked down at the sidewalk. "A couple grand."

Rourke let out a low whistle. "And this money is for what exactly?"

"Look, either lend me the money or forget it," Brandon snapped, and started to walk away.

"You're gambling," Rourke said, his voice low.

His little brother stopped and turned. "I'm in trouble."

Rourke swore. "Who is it you owe?"

Brandon shook his head.

"You tell me or I'm not going to help you."

"Kelly."

With an oath, Rourke raked a hand through his hair. "Burt Ace-up-his-sleeve friggin' Kelly? What the hell is wrong with you? Kelly has been fleecing ranch hands for years. Is he still with the VanHorn spread?"

Brandon nodded. "Look, don't go causing any trouble, all right? Just give me the money so I can pay him. You don't know what he's like. He'll kill me."

"*Kill* you?"

"He gets crazy sometimes. He told me last night that if I didn't come up with the money today I'd end up like Forrest Danvers," Brandon said.

Rourke froze. "You aren't making this up?"

"Do you think I'd lie about something like that?"

He hoped not as he studied his brother. Brandon had been nineteen when Forrest was murdered. "What do you know about Forrest's murder?"

"Nothing. Just what I told you," Brandon said.

"I'm going to pay your gambling debts," Rourke said carefully. "You're going to go back to the ranch and start helping the old man until you get a job."

Brandon started to argue but Rourke grabbed him by the collar.

"You are never going to gamble with Kelly again," Rourke continued, tightening his hold. "If I hear different, I'm going to kick your hide. Is that clear?"

"You sound like the old man," Brandon wheezed.

Rourke smiled. "Yeah, don't I. Too bad the old man didn't do the same to me. Maybe I wouldn't have gone to prison. But you and I, we're not having this discussion again." He let go of his brother. "We understand each other?"

Brandon rubbed his throat and nodded. "Let me pay Kelly. If you go out there—"

"I'll take care of it."

Brandon started to argue but wisely changed his mind.

"Go to the ranch, get cleaned up," Rourke said. "I won't mention this to J.T. when I call him to tell him you'll be working out there for a while."

"Look, can't I start tomorrow? I'm so hungover—"

"It will do you good," Rourke said. "I'll tell J.T. to put you on mending fence. You'd be amazed what the hot sun does to a hangover."

Brandon swore as he walked away. Rourke watched him drive out of town toward the ranch, thinking, damn if he hadn't become his father. The thought did nothing to improve his mood as he headed for his pickup.

ASA SPOTTED Rourke's pickup in front of the Longhorn just as Rourke started to climb behind the wheel. He should have bought his son a new truck, done something to let Rourke know he was glad he was out of prison, that he believed in his innocence, that he hadn't disinherited him and was sorry he'd ever threatened to.

But he'd done nothing, said nothing. He silently cursed himself for his stubborn pride or whatever it was that often made him act like an ass. Worse, that he couldn't even admit to acting like an ass to his own son.

"Rourke," Dusty called out the window, and motioned for him to wait.

Asa parked down the block from the café. "I'd just

as soon do this on my own," he said as Dusty opened her door.

"I'm sure you would," she said, ignoring him as she got out and started toward her brother.

Her mother's genes again, Asa thought as he followed her. He hadn't gone far when he saw a familiar figure come out of a building down the street. He stumbled, nearly fell.

"Dad," Dusty said, grabbing his arm to steady him. "Are you all right?"

He didn't answer, his attention still on the woman getting into the dark sports car.

"What is it?" Dusty said. "Dad?"

A truck pulled out, blocking his view of the woman, of the car and the license plate. The car sped away, giving him only a glimpse of blond hair.

"Who was that?" Dusty asked.

"What? No one. It's nothing."

"You look as if you just saw a ghost," Rourke said joining them.

Asa shook his head. "I'm okay." His voice broke. "I just need to watch where I'm going, that's all."

Dusty was eyeing him suspiciously. She glanced down the street toward where he'd been staring and looked as if she were about to say something when Rourke asked, "Do you need to sit down?"

Asa felt light-headed and realized he was shaking like a leaf.

"Dad hasn't been feeling so hot," Dusty said, always covering for him.

"I'm fine," Asa snapped. "I want you to come stay at the ranch, Rourke, where you belong."

Rourke lifted a brow and Asa immediately regretted his tone. Even Dusty groaned beside him.

"Son…" Asa tried again.

"Thanks for the…invitation, if that's what it was, but I'm staying at the cabin right now," Rourke said.

"Well, if you change your mind…" Asa said, feeling helpless. He could see that he'd disappointed Dusty and angered Rourke.

But as much as that distressed him, he was more upset over the woman he'd seen down the street. Or thought he'd seen.

"See you later," Rourke said to his sister before heading to his pickup.

Dusty went after him and Asa overheard her say, "Dad's been under a lot of stress lately but he really does want you to come home."

Asa leaned against the side of the building next to the Longhorn and tried to calm his racing heart. Stress? Hell, isn't that what everyone blamed nowadays? But could stress make you imagine a face that you'd spent years trying to forget?

"You could have been nicer," Dusty said not unkindly as she returned to take Asa's arm. Rourke looked their way as he drove off, headed south out of town. "Are you sure you're all right?" She sounded worried about him.

"I'm fine. You're right, I didn't eat yesterday. Let's get a burger on the way to pick up the grain. I'll let you drive."

That seemed to satisfy her. At least for the moment. But as she drove the truck down the street, like him, she appeared to be looking for the black sports car the blond woman had gotten into just before she disappeared from view.

ROURKE STOPPED at the bank, then drove south out of town. He couldn't believe that Kelly had the nerve to gamble with a McCall. Rourke's blood boiled at just the thought.

But it was the comment that Kelly had allegedly made about Forrest that had cooled Rourke down. Getting mad was one thing, but it took a cool head to get even. A lesson well learned at prison.

Just miles from the Wyoming border, he turned back up into the open country to the east through a huge log arch with the words *VanHorn Ranch* on a sign hanging from it.

Tacked on the post was a reward poster, the newer cardboard sign already weathered and worn but the lettering still readable: Reward For Any Information About The Vandalizing Of VanHorn Property.

VanHorn had been the first to allow coal-bed methane gas wells to be drilled on his property. The whole idea hadn't gone over well. In fact, someone had vandalized VanHorn's wells and drilling equipment. That had been before Rourke went to prison. Brandon had told him that VanHorn was still gunning for the culprit.

VanHorn had a long memory, never forgot a slight or a wrong. Mason was like Asa that way, Rourke thought, reminded of his own father.

The first VanHorn, Houston, had come to Montana

with Rourke's great-grandfather, Jed McCall. Both men had been cattlemen, born and bred. Then the families had a falling out, with the feud continuing each generation.

Rourke wondered what Houston VanHorn would think of his descendants allowing coal-bed methane drilling to be done on his land. Maybe Houston's ghost had vandalized the gas wells. At the very least the old man must be rolling in his grave to see the drilling rigs on VanHorn land. In that regard, Houston VanHorn had been like Asa.

Dust churned up behind the pickup as Rourke raced up the road. There were drilling units all along the road to the ranch house. In the distance, Rourke spotted a new well going in.

"There is money in methane," Brandon had written him in prison. "Dad's a fool to let it go to waste underground. It isn't like the wells hurt the land."

Good thing his brother wasn't here with him, Rourke thought. He'd have slugged him.

At the main ranch house, Rourke turned and drove down a short road to where a group of men were breaking a horse.

From the looks of the horse in question, it was a wild mustang from down in Wyoming. VanHorn had been rounding up the mustangs for years.

Rourke got out of his pickup. He didn't see Kelly in the group of men. He headed for the ranch office, cool and calm. At least on the surface.

He opened the door rather than knock. Burt Kelly looked up from behind a huge oak desk. The ranch foreman was tall and slim with a face like a ferret, eyes small and dark, his face pocked, his lips a thin mean line. He seemed surprised to see Rourke. It took something pretty big to get a McCall onto the VanHorn spread, given the long-running feud between the McCalls and VanHorns.

"Rourke McCall," Kelly said, and Rourke caught a flicker of worry in the older man's eyes. "I didn't think you'd have the guts to show your face around here again."

Rourke smiled. Kelly liked to goad people, make them angry, make them do something stupid. "You know why I'm here."

Kelly raised a brow. "I do?"

"I heard you're still a gambling man," Rourke said, his voice soft and deadly. "Want to make a wager as to why I'm here?"

Kelly laughed. "I'd win that one. Let me guess. Your little brother came whining to you. He's just like you, Rourke. A lousy poker player. Hotheaded and a poor loser."

Rourke smiled. "Some of us just don't play well with a liar and a cheat."

Kelly's face flushed. "Watch what you say, McCall, you're on VanHorn land now. If I pick up that phone, I can have a dozen men here within minutes. I don't think you want me to do that."

Rourke moved to the desk with such speed, Kelly rolled the chair back a few inches before he realized what Rourke had in mind.

Rourke picked up the phone and handed it to the foreman. "Better make that call, Kelly."

The older man just stared at him. "What is it you want, McCall?"

"You're never to deal another hand to any member

of my family. If I hear you do, I'll be back and it will be the last hand you deal."

"Don't you come in here threatening—"

"Here." Rourke took out the roll of cash he'd picked up at the bank on his way out of town. He counted out twenty-five hundred dollars, five hundred more than Brandon said he owed, onto the edge of the desk and raised a brow at Kelly. "Will that cover it?"

Kelly nodded and reached for the money. Rourke grabbed his hand, bringing the man out of his chair with a cry of pain. As Rourke came around the end of the desk, Kelly took an awkward swing at him with his left. Rourke grabbed that hand as well in a little grip he'd learned while behind bars.

"Which hand is it you use to deal from the bottom of the deck?" he asked Kelly quietly, putting pressure on both sets of fingers, forcing the man to drop to his knees. "The extra five hundred is for information. Did Forrest Danvers owe you money?"

Kelly groaned in pain.

"Yes or no," Rourke demanded.

"None of your damned business."

Rourke increased the pressure.

"Yes. He owed me over a grand in gambling debts."

"How did Forrest get into you for a grand? That's not like you, Kelly. He was just a ranch hand. It would take him months to pay you off."

Kelly looked up at him with hatred. Rourke applied a little more pressure to his hands and Kelly howled before blurting out, "Forrest had something going on the side. He would show up with a fat roll of money. I took him for at least ten grand."

"What was Forrest into for that kind of money?"

"I don't know. I swear."

Rourke put more pressure on Kelly's fingers.

"Gavin Shaw. Forrest and Gavin had something going on the side. That's all I know."

Blaze's stepbrother Gavin? Rourke let go of the foreman's hands. Kelly fell back against the wall beside his chair, cradling his hands in his lap as he bent over them. "You had Forrest killed for a thousand lousy dollars?"

"Hell no," Kelly said, finding his voice as feeling came back into his hands. "I'd have had him beat up or his legs broke. You know how I operate."

Rourke nodded solemnly. "I remember it well. But maybe this time you'd already beaten him up and he wasn't cooperating."

"Forrest was too big of a sucker. He would have come up with the grand and a whole lot more," Kelly said.

That's why the card shark would never have had Forrest killed, Rourke realized. Not the goose laying the golden eggs. "Who else would want Forrest dead?"

Kelly glared at him. "Besides you? How would I know?"

His eyes narrowed as if he were just catching up. "If you really didn't kill him—" Kelly sneered, his teeth dark from years of tobacco "—someone framed you and you thought it was *me?*" He laughed, his expression mean as the rattlesnake's. "I wish I *had* thought of it."

"Seen any rattlesnakes lately?" Rourke asked.

Kelly quit smiling, confusion taking its place. "Rattlesnakes?" He glanced around as if he thought Rourke might have let one loose in the office.

"Never mind. Where can I find Gavin," Rourke asked, and thought for a moment that he'd have to use force again to get Kelly to cooperate. But all the fight seemed to have gone out of the man. At least temporarily.

"Palmer Ranch," Kelly said, as he got up from the floor, rubbing his sore fingers as he did and watching the floor. He didn't seem to like the idea of rattlesnakes. Definitely not the type to put one in a gunnysack behind someone's pickup seat.

As Rourke left, he half expected Kelly to put in that call, but the VanHorn Ranch foreman preferred an ambush, not face-to-face confrontation. Also Rourke suspected Kelly didn't want trouble on the ranch. He didn't want his boss to know. What Mason VanHorn didn't see, Mason VanHorn let slide. There was no way Mason hadn't known for years about all the ranch hands Kelly had swindled. VanHorn had just turned a blind eye to it.

But not even Mason VanHorn could turn a blind eye to murder. Assuming Rourke was right, and Kelly was too greedy to kill his golden goose over a thousand bucks, then Kelly hadn't killed Forrest. At least not for money. But Kelly also didn't have the patience or the brains to frame him. Nor any reason to. More and more, Rourke was beginning to think Cassidy was right, and this wasn't about framing him but about Forrest, and Rourke was just an easy scapegoat.

If Forrest was into Kelly for a grand, then he might have had other debts, other enemies who weren't as charitable. Also, how was a ranch hand with no education or much ambition coming into so much money? Not legally, Rourke was sure.

So what was Forrest up to? And why did it have to be Blaze's stepbrother Gavin he'd been up to it with?

HOLT VANHORN LOOKED around his almost empty apartment and began to throw a few things into a suitcase. He didn't have much to pack. Everything had already been pawned in Billings, a couple hours away. People didn't know him down there and didn't ask questions.

He had what clothing he would need in the suitcase when his cell phone rang. He thought about letting it ring. But maybe it was his father. Maybe the old son of a bitch had had a change of heart. Not likely, but Holt had to take the chance. He was broke and he knew he wouldn't get far on what little money and gas he had in his car.

"Hello?" he asked hopefully.

"Do you have my money?"

"I told you I can't get any more money." Holt glanced around the room. He was busted and there was no way he could get more money from his old man.

"Then I guess I'll have to pay a visit to the cops."

Holt closed his eyes tight. "Tomorrow." He'd be long gone by tomorrow. "I'll get your money by tomorrow."

"You wouldn't be thinking about skipping out on me, would you, VanHorn? Because if you do that, I will go to the sheriff and then I'll go to your father. I wonder which one of them would track you down the fastest? We both know which one would be the hardest on you, don't we."

Holt slumped down on the edge of the bed. "I'll get your money."

"Damn straight you will. You can always rustle some more of your old man's cattle, right?"

"Give me until day after tomorrow," he said.

"Look out your window, Holt."

He froze for a moment, then moved slowly toward the window facing the street. As he pulled back the curtain, he heard laughter on the other end of the phone.

"I'm going to be your shadow until I get my money. Cross me and your father will be the first to know your secret." The line went dead.

Holt hung up the phone before he emptied out his suitcase. What was he going to do? He'd run out of places to get money and even if he got a job…

There was another way. At the mere thought, he began to shake. He closed his eyes and fought back the nausea that came with even the thought of blood.

Chapter Nine

Cassidy couldn't imagine how she could help Rourke find the person who had killed Forrest Danvers. It seemed impossible. The killer had remained hidden for eleven years.

And yet someone had put a rattlesnake in Rourke's pickup.

After the afternoon coffee break crowd cleared out, she told Arthur she had to run an errand and drove south out of Antelope Flats toward the Wyoming border.

There was no road sign that marked the border between Montana and Wyoming. The only way she knew she was in Wyoming was when the narrow two-lane highway turned red abruptly. From there to Sheridan, the road had been built with red earth.

She followed the red highway a few miles to the old Danvers place. Cecil Danvers lived in a small, old log cabin down by the river. His rusted-out pickup was parked in front and smoke curled up from the stovepipe sticking out of the roof.

The late summer air smelled of dried leaves and wood smoke as she walked to the front of the cabin and knocked on the weathered door. When there was no answer, she knocked again, a little harder.

The day was warm enough but she figured Cecil had built a fire in the woodstove because the cabin would be cold inside. She felt a sudden chill skitter up her spine and turned to find Cecil standing directly behind her.

Startled, she let out a cry of alarm.

He smiled, obviously pleased that he'd scared her. "What do *you* want?"

His brother Forrest hadn't been a bad-looking man, tall and slim with classic features. Cecil, though, was short and squat, thick-necked with a broad face, a predominant nose and thin lips stretched in a straight line across his stingy mouth.

"I was hoping to have a few words with you," she said, trying not to let him rattle her. Cecil had always made her a little nervous. She was questioning what had possessed her to come here by herself.

"I'm working," Cecil snapped. "I don't have time." He didn't look as if he'd been working, but she didn't argue the point.

"Maybe you could take a short break."

Cecil studied her a moment, then reached past her to open the cabin door. She could smell alcohol on his breath as he shoved the door open and moved past her. "Make it quick."

He went straight to the fridge and took out a beer. He didn't offer her one as she entered the dark cabin. Not that she would have taken it. The place was a mess, clothes strewn everywhere, dirty dishes on the counter and table and the smell of rotten food in the trash.

Cecil didn't offer her a chair, either. Even if there had been one that was cleared off enough to sit on, she wasn't staying that long. Now that she was here, she wasn't sure how to broach the subject of Forrest's murder.

"I know what you want," he said. "I heard you were helping Rourke try to pin my brother's murder on someone else." His laugh gave her a chill. "Good luck."

She wondered who would have told him, given that Rourke had only asked her to help him this morning. Blaze? She must have told him about Saturday night. It surprised her, but who else knew about Rourke's plan?

"I just wanted to ask you about that night. You were standing at the bar with Holt VanHorn, Easton Wells and Gavin Shaw when I walked in. You said something like, 'Now's your chance with Rourke. Blaze is dancing with Forrest.'"

Cecil took a long drink of his beer, avoiding her gaze. "I don't remember saying anything to you. You weren't even old enough to be in the bar. Les had no business letting you stay."

"A few minutes later the fight broke out and you left."

"I left before that." Not according to his testimony at the trial and collaboration by witnesses.

Cassidy realized this had been a total waste of time. Cecil couldn't even remember what he'd said under oath.

"Did you see anyone in the parking lot when you left?"

"I didn't see nobody."

"The killer could have been hiding in the parking lot

when Forrest left and followed him up Wild Horse Gulch."

He snorted.

"Why didn't you wait for Forrest to give you a ride home?" It was something she'd wondered about for years.

He took a drink of his beer and belched loudly. "I didn't feel like waiting around for him. You're wrong, there weren't nobody in the parking lot when we left."

We? "We? You just said when *we* left. I thought you hitchhiked home?"

He looked around the room as if something in it would help him out, then he made a resigned face and said, "Blaze gave me a ride as far as the turnoff to her daddy's ranch. So what of it?"

This isn't what he'd said at the trial. Was he lying now? Or eleven years ago?

"Blaze didn't leave until *after* the fight," she said.

"I was out in the parking lot smoking a cigarette," Cecil said defensively. "But I'd left the bar, all right?"

"You must have heard the ruckus inside." She hadn't meant to make her tone so accusatory.

His eyes narrowed. "It wasn't any of my business if Forrest wanted to get the piss kicked out of him. Didn't have nothing to do with me."

So much for brotherly love, she thought.

Cecil downed the last of his beer, smashed the beer can in his large paw of a hand and chucked it in the direction of the trash, missing. The can clattered to the dirty linoleum floor, not the first. Or the last.

He moved toward her and the door. "Time for you to go. McCall killed him and eleven years ain't near enough payment. If you were smart you'd mind your own business."

She backed up, slipping out the door. She could feel Cecil's cold, hateful glare drilling into her back like a steel bit as she walked to her car.

When she looked back over her shoulder, he was standing in the doorway, his eyes reminding her of the rattlesnake's in Rourke's pickup. As she got into her car, she hurriedly locked the doors and started the engine.

Cecil Danvers could have put the snake in Rourke's pickup. For that matter, Cecil could have killed his brother. Unless he had an alibi. Blaze. Was it possible she really had given him a ride as far as her father's ranch? But Blaze had been living in an apartment in town. Why had she gone out to the ranch? Maybe that hadn't been her destination. The next turnoff was Easton's family's place and the next—Cassidy felt a chill skitter across her skin. The next road past the ranch was Wild Horse Gulch.

BLAZE HEARD the faint tap on the window and looked up to see Yvonne Ames peering into the ADC office.

Blaze groaned, wishing she could have hidden before Yvonne saw her, but the woman was already going around to the front door.

Blaze had gone to school with Yvonne, but they'd never been friends, not that Blaze had had girl-type friends. Yvonne was one of those girls who'd always been chubby and unpopular with boys unless she put out.

"Hi," Yvonne said shyly as she opened the door to Blaze's office. "Got a minute?"

No. "What's up?" Blaze asked, motioning her in. She glanced at her watch to let Yvonne know she didn't have a lot of time.

Yvonne nervously took a chair across from Blaze's desk, dropping her purse, spilling the contents, then frantically trying to get everything back inside.

Blaze sighed and waited impatiently. "If this is about business, Easton will be back—"

"No," Yvonne said. "I wanted to see you." She got everything back inside her purse, clutching it to her, fingers nervously kneading the soft leather. "I heard Rourke McCall was back? I knew you'd see him when he got back." Yvonne swallowed. "I wondered if he said anything about me."

Was the woman serious? "Why would he say anything about *you?*"

She gave a slight shrug of one shoulder. "I just wondered."

"No, he didn't mention you at all." Yvonne must be losing her mind. Rourke wouldn't look twice at her.

Yvonne got to her feet. "I heard he was looking for the person who really killed Forrest," she said, still kneading her purse with nervous fingers.

"Of course, that's what he would say," Blaze snapped. "He has to make a show of proving his innocence." Rourke had lost her loyalty.

Yvonne's eyes widened. "You think he killed Forrest?"

Blaze shrugged. "I hate to think that any man I ever dated could be a killer...."

"Rourke wouldn't kill anyone," Yvonne said.

As if anyone cared what Yvonne thought. "Why

would you think Rourke might be asking about you?" Blaze asked, unable to let that go. "It wasn't like you were even at the Mello Dee the night of the murder."

Yvonne nodded and stepped toward the door. "I wrote him a couple of letters while he was in prison and sent him some cookies a few times, that's all."

Blaze stared at her. Why was Yvonne lying?

"Gotta go," Yvonne said, and made a hasty departure.

What was that about? Why would Rourke ask about *her?*

Blaze frowned as she watched Yvonne walk by the window. Yvonne shot a look back at the office. Yvonne looked as if she'd just put one over on her.

Blaze let out a curse. Cassidy had sworn on the witness stand during the trial that she'd overheard Forrest on the pay phone at the Mello Dee talking to a *woman* after his fight with Rourke, after Blaze had left, right before he left and was later murdered up Wild Horse Gulch.

The prosecutor had argued that Cassidy had no way of knowing if Forrest had been talking to a man or a woman. Cassidy had said Forrest called the person on the line "honey bun."

Blaze swore again. Forrest always called *her* honey bun, so she'd just assumed Cassidy had been lying to try to implicate her in the murder.

Now Blaze realized there *had* been another woman. What other reason would Yvonne have to stop by to ask if Rourke had inquired about her? Forrest had been two-timing her the night he was murdered? With Yvonne Ames? "You sorry bastard."

ON THE WAY THROUGH TOWN, Rourke stopped at the sheriff's office to see his brother.

"Dad just called," Cash said when Rourke walked in. "He wants everyone at dinner tonight. No arguments," he added before Rourke could decline. "And no I don't know what it's about, just that it must be a big deal or he wouldn't insist on having us all together in the same room."

Rourke knew the truth in that. He remembered too many meals that had turned into near knock-down-drag-out fights. Funny, but he almost missed them. He thought about how strangely his father had been acting today when he'd seen him and Dusty. His sister had said Asa hadn't been feeling well. "I'll be there. What time?"

"Six," Cash said, and looked relieved. "I heard Brandon is back out at the ranch. You know anything about that?"

Rourke shook his head.

"Yeah? You probably don't know anything about why Burt Kelly is acting oddly, either."

"Kelly?" Rourke echoed.

"I already heard that you were at the VanHorn Ranch this morning. Mason saw your pickup at the office and thought there might be a problem. He said Kelly was unusually subdued after you left."

"Really?"

Cash leaned his elbows on the desk and rubbed his temples with his fingers. "Want to tell me about it?"

Rourke knew he had to give his brother something. "Forrest owed Kelly money, a grand in gambling debts."

Cash sat up and let out a low whistle. "You thinking Kelly might have killed him over it?"

Rourke shook his head slowly. "But it makes me wonder if Forrest might have had other debts, other creditors who weren't so understanding. It also makes me wonder where Forrest got the money to start with. Kelly said he'd taken Forrest for ten big ones. Any idea where someone like Forrest Danvers would get that kind of money?"

Cash shook his head. The Danverses had been dirt poor for as far back as Rourke could remember. They were also uneducated and often in trouble with the law.

"I hope you're wrong about Kelly," Cash said. "I'd love to bust that bastard for murder."

Rourke nodded, knowing the feeling.

"So you didn't tear up the place? Kick Kelly's butt?" Cash sounded surprised.

"Prison taught me a few things," he said.

"I hate to think," Cash said and sighed. "But obviously prison didn't make you any smarter. Easton was just here. He's afraid you're going to get someone killed."

Blaze had told Easton about the Saturday-night plan. Dear Blaze.

"He told me some fool story about you reenacting the night Forrest was murdered. Someone could get killed."

"They did the last time. I was hoping you'd play Forrest," Rourke said.

"You can kiss my—"

"Don't worry." Rourke wondered why Easton had come whining to the sheriff. "Cassidy and I are going to find the killer before Saturday night."

"Cassidy? Dammit, Rourke, you aren't involving her in this, are you?"

"She's already involved, bro. And she's a big girl, she can make up her own mind about whether or not to keep helping me, all right?" He got to his feet. "By the way, those doughnuts you brought me this morning were wonderful."

Cash looked like he had a whole lot more to say but was biting his tongue. Obviously it was painful for him.

"Who do you think Easton was worried about getting killed?" Rourke asked, thinking of something the private investigator he'd hired had told him.

"You know Easton's been seeing Blaze."

Rourke smiled. He knew a whole lot about Easton. And Blaze. "Hasn't everyone been seeing Blaze?" He started for the door. "Even you, I hear."

"It wasn't a date," Cash called after him. "She asked for a ride home when her car didn't start."

Rourke was laughing as he left. It felt good. "See you at dinner."

"What's wrong?" Easton said from the doorway. All he'd heard was Blaze utter the words "You sorry bastard!" but he knew that look on her face only too well as she swung around from the window.

He would normally assume he was that bastard. Except something in her expression told him it wasn't him this time.

"Was that Yvonne Ames I saw leaving just now?" he asked. "What did she want?"

Blaze stared right through him for a moment. She shook her head as if trying to clear it. "She just stopped in to say hi."

He raised a brow. He could tell when Blaze was lying, without any effort, anymore.

"She invited me to lunch, wanted my advice. Man problems."

Blaze should have quit while she was ahead. He knew there was no way Yvonne would ask for her advice on anything. Maybe Blaze couldn't see it, but Yvonne hated her guts. He wondered what Blaze had done to her. Yvonne didn't seem the malicious type. He'd bet Blaze had taken some man from Yvonne that she was interested in. That was usually the case with the women who hated Blaze.

He walked over to his desk and put down his briefcase. "I think Yvonne is nice," he said, knowing it would set Blaze off.

"You would," she said under her breath but plenty loud enough for him to hear. "You should date her. If you haven't already."

He turned to look at her, unable not to smile. Blaze was so transparent sometimes. He noticed she'd changed out of that sexy blue dress she'd been wearing earlier. He wondered what that meant. Rourke must not be coming around. Is that what had put Blaze in this mood? Or was it Yvonne's real reason for stopping by that had set Blaze off? And what real reason had that been?

"Is everything all right?" he asked.

"Fine." She smiled but didn't put much effort into it.

"You seem a little on edge. I hope it isn't Rourke who's causing it," he said.

A flash of anger sparked in her eyes. "Rourke?" She let out a laugh. "Rourke has never caused me any trouble."

Uh-huh. Easton nodded, his mood picking right up until he remembered the trouble Rourke was causing him.

ROURKE DROVE OUT to the Palmer Ranch only to find that Blaze's stepbrother Gavin had taken the day off. He got the impression that Gavin had left that morning after getting a phone call warning him that Rourke was looking for him. Good old Kelly, no doubt.

On the way back to town, Rourke took the old road, slowing at the Mello Dee Supper Club and Lounge on the outskirts of town. The place looked just as it had eleven years ago. A roadhouse with a gravel parking lot, faded-paint building and blinking neon sign out front.

Rourke hoped to hell he and Cassidy found the killer before Saturday night as he pulled into the parking lot. He didn't want to come back here. There was only one other vehicle in the lot, a new blue pickup, so new it didn't even have plates yet.

He sat for a moment, just staring at the place, reliving memories that had haunted him for years. If he had just let Blaze dance with Forrest…or never gone up Wild Horse Gulch. But Cassidy was probably right. It wouldn't have made any difference once the killer had Rourke's gun with his fingerprints on it.

The place even smelled the way he remembered it. The supper club section was closed until five, but the bar was open. He glanced past the pool table. The place was dark. Except for the lit screen of a video poker machine in the corner. The single patron, a gray-haired man, sat on a stool in front of the machine, his back to him. The man didn't turn as Rourke took a stool at the bar.

Les Thurman was filling the beer cooler. He'd been behind the bar the night Forrest was murdered. Rourke had heard that he was still bartending even though he owned the place—just as he'd been the night Forrest was killed.

Les had always been cool, letting underage teens in to play pool or dance to the jukebox if the place wasn't busy. Which it often wasn't.

Les turned and blinked as if not sure he believed his eyes. He closed the cooler. "Rourke," he said warmly as he came over and shook his hand. "It's great to see you."

It was the most sincere greeting Rourke had had from locals and it warmed his heart more than he wanted to admit.

"What can I get you to drink?" Les asked. He was pushing sixty, his thick gray hair, his skin worn and wrinkled from years of ranching, before he sold the place to VanHorn and bought the Mello Dee some twelve or thirteen years ago.

"A beer would be great." Rourke watched Les pull a cold one out of the cooler, twist off the cap and place the bottle on a napkin in front of him.

Les leaned toward him, keeping his voice down as he glanced every so often at the man playing video poker. "I've thought about that night a million times over the years," he said before Rourke could bring up the subject. "I've regretted the hell out of not breaking up that fight sooner."

Rourke shook his head. "Nothing you did or didn't do that night had any bearing on what happened."

Les didn't look comforted by that.

"I've come to realize I brought a lot of it on myself."

Les didn't seem to hear him; he appeared lost in re-living the night. "I remember I was trying to close up. There were only a few of you kids hanging around. I started to shut down the jukebox at midnight but Blaze—"

"Wanted one last dance."

Les wagged his head. "I didn't see the harm in one more dance. She can be damned convincing when she wants to be."

Rourke nodded. Didn't he know it. "She was trying to make me jealous and, me being the fool I was, I let it get to me."

Les said nothing, clearly in agreement on all counts.

The guy at the poker machine got up, his back still to Rourke and the bar. Rourke watched him disappear down the hall to the men's room.

"I remember little about the fight, but Cassidy said she thought some of the guys at the bar were goading me on," he said, turning his attention back to the bar.

Les raised a brow at Cassidy's name. "Yep, Easton. Cecil." He dropped his voice even lower, "Holt VanHorn. They were giving you a hard time, that's for sure. They even gave Cassidy a hard time when she came in. They were trying to stir up anyone they could that night." He shook his head. "I'm sorry as hell about what happened."

Rourke drank his beer in the silence that fell between them. Everything about the place reminded him of that night eleven years go. He doubted Les had changed a thing. It was as if time had stood still here.

The sound of the video poker machine in the corner broke the long silence.

Rourke looked toward the man seemingly intent again on his game. "He must be winning."

Les shook his head. "Losing," he whispered. "Usually plays a lot better. Must be distracted trying to hear what we're saying."

The man turned as if on cue.

Rourke was stunned to see that it was Mason Van-Horn. Mason had changed drastically in the past eleven years, his dark hair now completely white, his face lined. He looked much older than his contemporary, Rourke's father, Asa.

Mason didn't seem all that surprised to see him. Obviously Les had been right about VanHorn trying to hear their discussion.

"Welcome home," Mason said, sliding off his stool to walk over to him. "Les, give Rourke another beer. Put it on my tab."

"Thanks just the same," Rourke said, and downed some of his beer, suddenly just wanting to get out of there. He could feel the hotheaded younger Rourke bubbling under his skin, the one who used to make scenes and get into barroom brawls.

Mason VanHorn pulled up the stool next to him at the bar and motioned to Les to make him another drink. Rourke saw Les's expression. He didn't like VanHorn any better than Rourke did. But then Les might have even more reason to hate VanHorn. There'd been talk years ago that VanHorn had cheated Les out of his ranch, forced him to sell.

"I'll have to go get another bottle of Scotch," Les said, making it clear he was put out.

Mason didn't seem to notice. "So how is your father?" he asked Rourke, as if he and Asa were old friends instead of lifelong adversaries. "Probably pretty much semi-retired like me, I guess."

"He's fine," Rourke said, not looking at him.

"I haven't seen him in town much," Mason said, and turned his empty drink glass in his fingers as he waited for Les to come back. "I heard he had a heart attack a while back. I hope he's feeling all right."

Rourke could feel the heat, the anger like a second skin just beneath his. "How is Holt these days?"

Mason bristled. "Fine."

Brandon had told him that Mason and Holt had had a falling-out and Holt had moved into town. Right after Rourke went to prison. "Some kind of bad blood there," Brandon had said. "No one seems to know what it was about."

Les came from the back with a bottle of Scotch and took his time mixing Mason a drink.

"Holt's just fine," Mason repeated and took a swallow of his old drink, all water by now. "I'll tell him you asked about him."

"You do that," Rourke said, finishing his beer. Les motioned that his beer was on the house as he set Mason's mixed drink in front of him.

Rourke nodded his thanks and left a tip as he slid off the stool.

"It was good seeing you," Les said.

"You, too," Rourke said.

"Again, I'm sorry the way things turned out," Les said, sounding like he meant it.

Rourke tried not to look at Mason VanHorn. He knew he should just walk away before he said or did something he would regret. Mason knew damned well that his foreman fleeced every cowhand in the county when he got the chance. But Rourke knew that was only part of the reason he despised the man. His dislike was in-herited—a family grudge that went back to his grand-father's time but had continued with his own father and Mason.

Rourke wasn't even sure what all the VanHorns had done to start the feud between the two families. What-ever it was it ran deep. Probably a battle over land. Wasn't that usually the case? That or a woman.

He glanced over at Mason. "On second thought, don't bother to give Holt my regards. I'll be looking him up myself."

He noted Mason's uneasy look, then turned and walked out. He was almost to his pickup, when he saw the piece of white folded paper stuck under his wind-shield wiper.

A sense of déjà vu made him sick to his stomach. Like a sleepwalker, he moved toward the pickup and plucked the note from under the windshield, unfolding the paper just as he had the night of Forrest's murder.

He thought he could feel someone watching him from inside the bar. Mason.

He stared down at the words scrawled on the note: *Leave well enough alone or join Forrest.* He balled up the note, turning to look back at the bar. The late-after-noon sun glinted off the windows, making it impossi-ble to see inside. Mason had left the video poker machine supposedly to go to the men's room. He could have slipped out the back door easy enough and put the note under the wiper.

Rourke realized he could also have been followed to the bar. He hadn't been watching for a tail, hadn't even thought he needed to. He wouldn't make that mistake again.

Rourke got into his truck, tossed the note to the floor and started the engine, shaking inside from anger.

Did someone really think he could be scared off by a rattlesnake or a stupid note?

Chapter Ten

Everyone was already in the family dining room standing around waiting when Rourke walked in just before six.

He took his old spot across from J.T., and for a moment he felt as if he hadn't been gone eleven years, as if he'd never been to prison, as if it had all been a bad dream.

"You want to tell us what this is about?" J.T. asked his father after they were all seated.

"Can't a father have his family to dinner without there being some big announcement?" Dusty asked.

They all ignored her, instead waiting for Asa to tell them what was going on.

Rourke looked down the table at his father. Asa had been acting strangely, but Rourke figured it had something to do with him getting out of prison. He just hoped to hell that wasn't what this dinner was about as he watched Martha and several new cook's assistants serve the food.

"Come on, what's going on?" J.T. demanded. "You practically jump out of your skin every time the phone rings."

Asa was pushing his food around on his plate and didn't seem to hear.

"Dad?" Cash said.

His father looked up in surprise. "I'm sorry, you want the roast?" he asked, reaching for the large platter.

"No," J.T said. "I asked what the hell is bothering you. If something's going on we should know about—"

The doorbell rang. Asa knocked over his water glass as he stumbled to his feet.

"Martha's got it," J.T. said.

Rourke, like all the others, was staring at his father. Asa had gone pale and, even from where Rourke sat, he could see that his father was shaking.

Martha appeared in the doorway. Like Asa, she seemed upset.

Rourke was on his feet. "Martha, what is it?" He'd barely gotten the words out of his mouth when a woman appeared in the doorway. She was blond, somewhere in her late fifties although she could have passed for much younger. She had the palest, clearest blue eyes he'd ever seen—even paler than his own.

Although he'd been too young to remember his mother, he knew that's who she was. Just as he realized in that instant of absolute silence before all hell broke loose that his father had lied about her death.

"What the hell is going on?" J.T. demanded.

Asa didn't seem to hear him. "As usual, Shelby, your timing is horrendous."

Her laugh was magnificent and Rourke thought he remembered it, that wonderful joyous tinkle of laughter that seemed to light up the entire house.

"Oh, Asa, you old goat, you know you love surprises," she said, looking around the table, her blue eyes seeming hungry as if she couldn't get enough of each of them.

Asa was looking at Shelby, a mixture of anger and awe, Rourke thought. He could practically feel the chemistry between them.

He looked over at his sister. The resemblance was uncanny between Dusty and Shelby and he could see that Dusty hadn't missed it. He let out a low oath and shook his head. He'd always suspected Dusty was his half sister but now it was clear who her mother had been.

Everyone was talking at once, just like the old days before the knock-down-drag-out fights began.

Shelby walked over to Asa, her eyes tearing as she kissed his old weathered cheek. "Something tells me this is going to be some story," Rourke said under his breath.

"Everyone settle down," Asa ordered loudly. "Martha, break out the good bourbon. Now you know the truth. Your mother is alive."

"No kidding," J.T. snapped.

"*Our* mother?" Dusty demanded.

Asa nodded, turning his attention to her, his expression softening. "You're a McCall in every sense of the word."

Rourke could see that Dusty was as angry as her brothers now. "You lied to me all these years?"

"I need to speak with your mother alone." Asa looked to Shelby, his expression as close to a plea as Rourke had ever seen.

"If you'll excuse us," Shelby said.

J.T. and Cash started to argue.

"We'll only be a moment," she said. "Then I want to talk to all of you."

Asa closed the dining-room door firmly behind them.

J.T. was the first to speak. "What the hell? Did any of you…" He broke off, seeing that none of them had a clue. "Someone please tell me why we've been putting flowers on her grave for the past thirty years?"

"You think they are still married?" Dusty asked Rourke.

"Must be."

"Where has she been?" Brandon asked into the stunned silence. "Why didn't she let us know she was alive?"

"Amnesia," Dusty said. "I read about this woman who was on her way to the grocery store and bumped her head and they found her years later in Alaska or someplace."

"Our mother didn't have amnesia," Cash said. "Unless it comes and goes. Dad just said you were his daughter with her."

Dusty frowned. "Why did he let me believe that he adopted me?"

"Who knows what else the old man has been hiding from us," Rourke said, and chuckled to himself. Just when he thought his father couldn't surprise him.

"How could he keep a secret like this?" J.T. said. "I've seen our mother's obituary from the newspaper. There's an elaborate tombstone on her grave."

"*Everyone* thought she was dead, not just us," Rourke agreed.

J.T. shook his head. In the silence that fell between them, they could hear raised voices in the den.

"She is beautiful, isn't she," Brandon said.

Rourke nodded and looked at Dusty, who was fuming at her end of the table. "Just like her daughter."

Tears welled in Dusty's eyes as she looked at him, then quickly excused herself and disappeared into the hall powder room.

"I could kill the son of a bitch for hurting *her*," Rourke said.

"You've killed enough people," J.T. snapped.

"It's just an expression," Cash said.

"Not one Rourke should be using," J.T. said.

"Okay, let's not argue," Brandon said. "This is stressful enough as it is. Let's not turn on each other."

"Brandon's right," Cash said. "If anything, we need to pull together."

"You're right," J.T. said. "Can you imagine what will happen when the news hits town?"

They all groaned.

"What if she isn't staying?" Dusty said from the doorway. They hadn't noticed that she'd returned.

"What if she is?" J.T. said.

They fell silent as they heard the den door open and close, then footfalls.

Asa appeared in the doorway. Shelby wasn't with him. "Your mother wants to talk to you all in the den, but first there is something I need to tell you." He cleared his throat. He was visibly shaking and his voice broke as he said, "Your mother is back."

They all let out a nervous laugh.

"No kidding," Rourke said.

"Back from the dead?" J.T. asked.

"Back?" Dusty echoed. "You mean she's going to be living with us? Where has she been?"

"Shouldn't this have come up years ago?" J.T. joined in.

Asa raised one hand and picked up his glass of bourbon with the other. He drained his glass. "I think I'd better explain."

BLAZE WAS WORKING LATE AGAIN when she looked up to see her brother Gavin pass by the window. He slowed, looked in, saw her and quickened his step.

Blaze heard the front door open and braced herself, curious and yet dreading seeing her brother. She'd heard that Gavin had left the VanHorn Ranch and was now working on the Palmer Ranch. She wondered how that had happened. Knowing her brother, she had a pretty good idea.

"Hey," he said, coming into her office and closing the door behind him. He wore old jeans and boots, a soiled shirt and hat.

"Why are you so dirty?" she asked, hoping no one had seen him come in.

"I've been *working,*" he said, sounding irritated with her, but quickly added in a more civil tone, "How are you?"

As if he cared. "Fine." If he wanted money, he was out of luck. She used all that she made and then some—and didn't even live that well.

He looked around the office. "Not bad."

"Not mine," she said.

He turned to grin at her. "You think I came by to bum

you for money?" He laughed as if the idea were ludicrous. They both knew better. "Can't a brother stop in to see his sister?"

*Step*brother. She hadn't been all that thrilled when her mother died and her father had remarried a woman named Kitten—who named their child Kitten, anyway?—and Kitten had a son who was two years younger than Blaze.

"What do you want, Gavin?" she asked, cutting to the chase.

"Have you seen Rourke?"

Rourke? "Of course."

He looked relieved. "I figured you two would get back together."

She didn't correct him. "What do you want with Rourke?"

"I heard he was looking for me." Gavin didn't sound happy about that. Was there some reason he shouldn't be?

First Yvonne and now her brother? "Why would he want to see you?"

He shrugged. "I thought he might have told you what he wanted."

She stared at her brother. "You never told me why you left VanHorn."

He glanced toward the street. "That's old news."

"He fired you."

Gavin swung his head around to glare at her. "Why would you say that?"

"What did you do?" she demanded impatiently.

"There was a misunderstanding," he said, looking away again. "Over a couple of his cattle."

"You were rustling his cattle?" She hated the admiration she heard in her tone.

He grinned. "I got a hundred head before I was caught."

"I'm surprised VanHorn didn't kill you."

"It was close," he admitted.

"And you still got on at the Palmer Ranch?" This surprised her. Under normal circumstances, his actions would have him blacklisted from every ranch around.

He shrugged again. "VanHorn gave me a good recommendation. How do you beat that?" He glanced again to the street.

This time she followed his gaze and saw Holt VanHorn sitting in a pickup across the street.

"Do you need to go out the back way?" she asked.

Her stepbrother laughed. "Naw, Holt's waiting for me. I gotta go."

Her brother was running with Holt VanHorn? This could explain why VanHorn had let the cattle rustling go. He must have thought his son was involved.

"When will you see Rourke?" he asked.

She had worked late again tonight hoping he'd come by. He'd disappointed her for a second time. "He's tied up tonight." She just hoped it wasn't with Cassidy. "Did you want me to give him a message?"

"See if you can find out what he wants."

She eyed him. "Why would he want to talk to you?"

Gavin shrugged. "Not a clue."

"You know he's determined to find out who killed Forrest," she said.

"I know." He met her gaze then and she saw fear, but she couldn't be sure if it was for her or for himself.

"I ADMIT IT. I lied," Asa said, the words like stones in his mouth. He looked around the table, hoping to find one of his offspring who might show him some compassion, some understanding. He saw nothing but anger, confusion, suspicion. Not even Dusty gave him the least bit of encouragement.

He reached for the bottle of bourbon to pour himself another drink, but J.T. moved it out of his reach.

"Shelby and I were wrong for each other from the very beginning," he said.

There was a burst of laughter around the table. "What? You didn't notice until after your fourth son was born?" Rourke said.

"It was a love-hate relationship," Asa said, realizing how ill-equipped he was to explain this to them. He'd had trouble explaining it to himself for years.

Maybe he should throw himself on their mercy. He looked around the table. It would be like throwing himself to wolves.

"We realized we couldn't live together. She would have to leave, but I didn't want you kids thinking your mother had just left you—"

"She *did* just leave us," Cash said.

"—so I faked her death."

"Unbelievable," J.T. said.

"And illegal," Cash added.

"You don't understand," Asa said, and groaned. "I wanted to protect you kids."

"Protect us from our mother?" Brandon asked.

Asa looked at his youngest son, the one most like Shelby. "Protect you from divorce, a divided family."

"And how do you explain me?" Dusty said, sounding close to tears.

Asa looked down the table at her, wanting to shelter her but there was no holding back now. If he didn't tell them, Shelby would.

"You were a love child, just as I told you," he said quietly. "Shelby and I...got together to talk and—"

"When was this?" J.T. demanded.

"Seventeen years ago, give or take nine months," Rourke said.

"That trip down south you took," J.T. said, as if suddenly remembering. He shook his head. "Has anything you've ever told us been the truth?"

Asa sighed and pinched the bridge of his nose. He straightened to his full height. "I did what I had to do. Someday when you're a parent—"

"Bull," Brandon said, and got to his feet. "I want to hear what my mother has to say about all this."

The rest were on their feet. As Rourke passed him, Asa saw that at least one son expected there was more to the story.

The moment they were gone, Asa grabbed the bourbon and poured himself a stiff drink. He was going to need it. Shelby was back. God help them all. At least the truth was out. He told himself it couldn't get any worse than this, but he knew better. When the past came back to haunt you, you never knew what other ghosts it brought with it.

SHELBY LOOKED UP as Rourke and his siblings entered the den. She'd been standing by the fireplace, obviously waiting for them.

Rourke closed the door firmly and, as the others moved deeper into the room, he stayed by the door.

His first impression of her hadn't done her justice. She was beautiful. He'd always wondered where their looks had come from. Obviously from their mother.

"Dad just told us how he faked your death to protect us from the truth," J.T. said to her. "Now we'd like to hear the truth."

She studied her children one by one, her gaze locking with Rourke's as if she was acknowledging he would be the hardest one to sell her story to. Her smile slipped away.

"Your father and I couldn't get along. One of us had to go."

"Why didn't you send *him* packing?" Cash asked.

"Asa would never leave his ranch. I had no idea how to run a ranch and you were his sons. Sons need a father."

"And daughters?" Dusty asked.

"So you just agreed to leave?" J.T. said.

"It was a sacrifice I felt I had to make," she said softly, her attention on Dusty. "As hard as it was for me. I felt your lives would be better without me than with me in town. I didn't want you torn between two quarreling parents like in so many divorces."

"So you're divorced?" Cash asked.

"No," she said. "That was another stigma we didn't want you to have to live with, and I knew I would never remarry."

"Marriage to Asa was that bad?" Rourke said from his spot by the door.

She smiled at him. "I knew I would never love anyone the way I loved your father."

"Uh-huh," Rourke said.

"So you went along with his plan to fake your death, right down to the memorial service and the gravestone at the cemetery?" Cash demanded.

She straightened. "It seemed like a way to put an end to it at the time."

"What about me?" Dusty demanded. Rourke could hear the anger and hurt in her voice. She sounded close to tears.

"Oh, honey," Shelby said, and took a step toward her but stopped as if seeing something in Dusty's eyes that warned her not to come any closer. "Your father and I got together to discuss a financial matter and…" She waved a hand through the air. "I know you're all angry and think we acted irresponsibly."

There were sounds of agreement around the room.

"Not to mention illegally," Cash piped up.

"But we love each other. You were all born of that love," Shelby said. "We just couldn't live together and that's why I went away, planning never to return."

"But you have returned," Rourke said.

"Yes." She looked across the room to him again. "I had to come home."

"Why now?" J.T. asked.

"Why not years ago, when we needed you?" Brandon said.

She shook her head, tears welling in her blue eyes. "I wanted to, desperately. But I never knew how long Asa and I would be able to stay together without killing each other. I couldn't do that to young children."

"So you waited until we were old enough to understand?" Rourke suggested, knowing there was a whole lot more to this story.

"That's partly it," she said, as if choosing her words carefully. "Your father and I need to work out some things."

"Financial things?" Rourke asked.

"It isn't what you think," she said. "It's between your father and I."

He'd heard enough. He turned and opened the door. If he hurried, he could catch Cassidy before the café closed.

"Are you staying?" he heard Dusty ask her mother as he headed down the hall toward the front door. He caught a glimpse of his father still at the dining-room table, steadily depleting the bottle of bourbon in front of him.

Rourke didn't catch his mother's answer. He didn't need to. Shelby wouldn't be staying. She was the kind of person whose first instinct when things went bad was to run away from it. Rourke knew now who he'd inherited it from.

Asa heard the front door open and close five times, heard several vehicles start up, heard angry voices in deep discussion out on the porch and figured Rourke and Cash had left. The other three were tearing him to shreds on the porch.

He poured himself another drink. Not even the alcohol was going to work tonight.

At the sound of her soft footfalls, he looked up. "How did it go?" he asked, already knowing the answer.

Shelby sat down heavily in a chair next to him. He pushed the bottle of bourbon toward her.

She had never been a drinker, so he was surprised when she poured a shot into the glass and downed it. She shuddered, eyes closed, tears beading her lashes.

When she opened her pale blue eyes, he felt a start, just as he had the first time he'd seen her. His heart ached just looking at her. He'd loved this woman all of his life, and not even the bad years or the long time apart could dull that all-enveloping love.

Nor could they have been more wrong for each other.

"You think they'll ever forgive me?" she asked.

"Yes," he said without hesitation. "They're just angry right now. They think you abandoned them."

"I did."

He shook his head. "You and I know that isn't true."

"I could have put up more of a fight."

Again he shook his head. "It wouldn't have done any good. You and I would have ended up killing each other. And imagine how many more children we would have had."

She smiled at that. "They are all so wonderful, aren't they?"

He started to tell her that *wonderful* wouldn't be the word he would choose for their pigheaded, contrary offspring, but he said, "Yes, they're wonderful. Dusty is the spitting image of you."

Tears welled again in her eyes. She discreetly wiped at them. "There will be an uproar when word gets out."

He nodded. "Why are you back, Shelby? I thought we had a deal," he asked, even though he feared he already knew, had known, the moment he saw her in town.

She reached silently to cover his hand with her own. As she squeezed his hand, tears spilled down both her cheeks. "You know why, Asa."

He nodded. Some secrets were impossible to keep.

Chapter Eleven

As Rourke pulled up in front of the Longhorn Café, he felt a rush of relief at the mere sight of Cassidy inside the café. He'd made it just in time. She was putting up the Closed sign as he got out of his pickup.

The rush of feeling surprised him and he realized it wasn't just his temper he'd learned to control in prison. He'd put a lid on a lot of other emotions, as well.

Cassidy spotted him, seeming surprised, as she opened the door. After everything that had happened today, she was like a breath of fresh air.

"Is everything all right?" she asked, studying his face.

He smiled at her. "Could we maybe—" he glanced at one of the booths "—talk?" It surprised him how much he was hoping she'd say yes. He couldn't think of any other place he wanted to be right now than here with Cassidy.

She didn't hesitate. "Sure. Want something to eat or drink?"

"Coffee would be nice if you still have any or I could make some."

"You?" she asked with a laugh.

"I worked in the prison cafeteria before I got on at the ranch," he said. "You'd be surprised at all my talents."

Did she blush? She pointed him toward the coffeepot while she went to close the blinds. As she was closing the last one, he saw her hesitate and looked past her to see Blaze sitting in her office across the street obviously waiting for someone. Guess who.

Task completed, Cassidy turned back to him.

"Where do you want to sit?"

She pointed to a booth, waited as he slid in, then sat down across from him. Their knees bumped. She jerked as if hit with a cattle prod. Or maybe she was just startled and he'd imagined the electrical current that shot through him.

"Did something happen today since I've seen you?" she asked, sounding worried.

"It's been quite the day," he said. He recounted what his brother Brandon had said about Forrest's gambling. He told her about his visit to the VanHorn Ranch and Kelly, leaving out how he'd gotten Kelly to talk to him. And finished up with his visit to Les Thurman at the Mello Dee.

"He told me you were right about the guys at the bar egging me on during the fight."

Cassidy nodded. Was that what he'd wanted to tell her? That she'd been right?

He looked at her across the table. "Cassidy—" The coffee machine shut off noisily.

It was a knee-jerk reaction. She started to slide out of the booth to go get the coffee.

"Let me," he said, and got up.

Slowly she lowered herself into the booth again. Her

heart was hammering in her chest. What had he been about to say?

"Here," he said, returning with the pot and two cups. He filled hers, then his, and took the pot back.

She cupped her hands around the cup, needing the warmth. She was staring down at the coffee when he returned. She didn't look up until the silence was too much for her. "You were saying?"

He shook his head as if he couldn't remember or it didn't matter anymore. She felt her heart drop. She had a feeling it did matter. A lot.

"Mason VanHorn was at the Mello Dee," he said.

She knew about the bad blood between the families. Not what had caused it, just that Asa and Mason couldn't be in the same room together.

Rourke seemed to hesitate. "My father called a family dinner tonight to make an announcement." He drew away to stare down into his coffee but not before she'd seen that instant of vulnerability in his blue eyes.

So unlike Rourke, she told herself she must have imagined it. "What was the announcement?"

"He didn't get to it before my mother walked in."

She stared at him, not sure if it was some kind of morbid joke or she just wasn't getting it.

"You heard me right. My mother. Shelby Ward McCall. It seems her death was exaggerated."

Cassidy gasped. "But your brothers put flowers on her grave every Sunday."

He nodded. "I guess she and my father cooked up her death thinking it would be better for us kids to believe her dead than divorced."

"That's screwball thinking if I've ever heard any," she said, then wished she could bite her tongue.

He laughed. "My thought exactly." He shook his head, his gaze moving gently over her face. "I would suspect my father paid her to go, threatening to take us kids and leave her penniless. That sounds more like him. You want to hear the real kicker? Dusty is theirs. She's our biological sister. It seems at some clandestine meeting to discuss finances, Dusty was the result."

Cassidy wouldn't have believed it if it hadn't been Asa McCall. *"Amazing."*

Rourke nodded in agreement.

"Why did she come back if they had an arrangement?"

"That is the question, isn't it," he said with a shrug. He looked worried.

"Didn't she say?" Cassidy asked.

"Not really, but my father didn't seem all that surprised to see her."

"Maybe they're getting back together," she suggested.

Rourke let out an oath. "I hope not. I was pretty young when she supposedly died, but I remember how the two of them fought. I could barely remember what my mother looked like, but I remember their infamous arguments. My father said they had a love-hate relationship. I doubt that has changed."

She sipped her coffee. "Good." She motioned to the coffee when he seemed confused.

He nodded and they fell into an uneasy silence.

Had he just wanted to tell her about his mother coming back from the dead? Or was there something else on his mind?

"I'm sorry," he said after a few minutes.

She looked up in surprise.

"I was so quick to blame you for what happened eleven years ago," he said. "I'm sorry."

She waved off his apology. "I would have thought the same thing. I did some investigating on my own today," she said. He seemed surprised. "I went out to see Cecil."

"Cassidy, you shouldn't have—"

"I figured it might be safer for me to talk to Cecil Danvers than for you," she said. "He was the one who'd goaded me about you and Blaze that night at the bar. He left when the fight broke out, which is odd in itself, but today he told me that he got a ride partway home."

Rourke put down his coffee cup.

"Cecil says he caught a ride with Blaze," Cassidy said.

Rourke stared at her. "That's not what he said in court. Not what Blaze said, either."

She nodded. "He could be lying. But I thought it was interesting because he said she dropped him off on the highway at the turnoff to her father's ranch—just up the road from Wild Horse Gulch."

Rourke let out an oath.

"There is just one problem. If Cecil is telling the truth, then the woman Forrest was talking to on the pay phone at the Mello Dee after your fight couldn't have been Blaze."

"He was meeting someone else," Rourke said, and let out a laugh.

She nodded. "It could explain why Cecil didn't wait around for a ride home with him."

"You think Cecil knew who his brother was meeting?" he asked.

She shrugged. "I wonder why Blaze lied about going straight home."

Rourke let out a low whistle. "If Cecil is telling the truth, this puts a whole new spin on things."

"You believed, the past eleven years, that Forrest was meeting Blaze, too," she said in surprise.

"Knowing Blaze, it was definitely a possibility. Especially after I heard that Forrest had come into some money."

Cassidy laughed. "Maybe you know Blaze better than I thought."

"You think Blaze could have killed Forrest?" he asked.

"I think she's capable of it. Aren't we all?"

He raised a brow. "I can't imagine you hurting a fly."

"You think I couldn't kill someone who was hurting someone I loved, well you're just wrong, Rourke McCall."

"Whoa," he said, holding up his hands in surrender. "Sorry for even insinuating you weren't a killer."

She took a breath, regretting her outburst. "It's just that people in this town think I'm a Goody Two-shoes without any of the normal feelings that everyone else has."

He laughed. It was a wonderful sound that she realized she had missed desperately. "I don't think of you as a Goody Two-shoes."

She eyed him suspiciously. "You're just saying that to make me feel better."

He laughed again. "You are one strange woman, Cassidy Miller. Strange and quite…unique and wonderful."

Her cheeks flamed. She lowered her eyes then felt his fingers, warm under her chin as he raised her face again.

"I mean it," he said. "There is no one like you."

Not exactly what she'd hoped to hear him say all these years. She returned to their discussion. "What makes you so sure Blaze didn't kill him?"

"What was her motive?" he asked, making her realize he'd already considered Blaze a suspect. Maybe he wasn't so clueless when it came to Blaze after all.

"Does Blaze need a reason?"

He smiled at that. "Believe me, if Blaze killed him, she had her reasons."

"Maybe he was threatening to tell you about the two of them," she suggested.

"Then why dance with him at the Mello Dee?" Rourke said, shaking his head. "Blaze loves to make men jealous."

He had a good point. "You suspected Forrest and Blaze were sneaking around, didn't you."

His eyes narrowed, a muscle in his jaw tightening. "I know you think I'm a complete fool, but I'm not so dumb that I didn't suspect she was seeing Forrest behind my back."

She shook her head. "That's why you were just spoiling for a fight when you tried to cut in on the dance floor."

"I'm not that man anymore," Rourke said, realizing it was true. The man he was now wouldn't fight over Blaze or go chasing after her up Wild Horse Gulch or any other place. He got up to refill their coffee cups. "I need you to tell me everything you can remember about the days leading up to the murder and that night, and I need you to be honest with me."

"I thought I've been painfully honest with you."

He smiled. "Very painful. You've made me take a hard look at the person I used to be."

"But you still aren't sure I didn't frame you," she said, her voice sounding small.

He shook his head. "I wanted to believe it, because it made things easy. I don't anymore."

"What changed your mind?"

"You." His gaze locked with hers. "I never knew you, Cassidy. If I had…" He waved a hand through the air. "I was obviously oblivious to a great deal. I can't help but wonder what else I missed, you know?"

She nodded slowly. She had a great face, big brown eyes and a smile that had a stunning effect.

"So where do we start?" he asked her.

"I guess with what we know. Whoever killed Forrest didn't do it on the spur of the moment," she said. "The killer planned it maybe even before he or she took your gun."

"Planned for me to take the blame—if not get even with me," he said.

She nodded. "It would help if you knew when your gun went missing."

"The night of my birthday party, everyone who was at the Mello Dee the night Forrest was killed, was also in the house." Not to mention that Blaze had access to it in the weeks before the murder since he'd kept the gun on a shelf in his bedroom. How stupid that he hadn't realized the gun could be more than a sentimental souvenir to someone with murder on his mind. Or her mind.

"Didn't Blaze throw that party for you at your ranch?"

"You make a good argument," he admitted. Maybe he had been blind when it came to Blaze.

"The party was a week before the murder," Cassidy said. "Let's say that was when the gun disappeared. So our suspects are those same people who were at the Mello Dee the night of the murder, because no one else could have known about Forrest's plans to go up Wild Horse Gulch." Cassidy frowned. "I take that back. Blaze's stepbrother Gavin wasn't at the party now that I think about it."

"You're right. I vaguely remember something about a fight?"

Cassidy nodded. "At the bunkhouse out on the Van-Horn ranch where Forrest and Gavin had both been working."

"So Gavin Shaw couldn't have taken the gun at the party."

"But he was at the Mello Dee that night," she said.

"The only other person we can't be sure about is whomever Forrest called from the Mello Dee pay phone and asked to meet him up the gulch," Rourke pointed out.

"So the people who were at my party and the bar were Blaze Logan, Easton Wells, Cecil Danvers and Holt VanHorn," Cassidy said.

"What we don't have is motive."

"But we do know that the killer is patient," he said. "He stole the gun, waited at least a week until he saw his chance. He doesn't do things on impulse. Or *she*," he added. "Doesn't sound like Blaze, does it?"

"No. But I really am worried about you, Rourke. If that rattlesnake had come out while you were driving, you could have wrecked the truck and been killed."

He shook his head. "It was just a warning. The killer is waiting to see what we come up with. I'm not sure he has the stomach to kill again. Remember, he has to find someone to blame it on again."

"How do you know the killer hasn't been planning this for eleven years?"

"I don't know what I would do without your help. I mean it. For eleven years, I couldn't even imagine that Forrest's death was about anyone but me, because it sent me to prison. But I was the perfect scapegoat, wasn't I."

"The wild McCall?" she asked with a laugh. "Every father in this county warned his daughters about you and your brothers."

"You didn't listen, did you?"

She sat back down and dropped her gaze to her lap. He'd embarrassed her. It surprised him the way her cheeks flushed, and when she looked up, her eyes were bright. He felt his breath come a little quicker.

She looked away and bit her lower lip.

"Anyway, thanks to you, I feel like we're making progress," he said into the tense silence that stretched between them.

"Just be careful," she said, finally looking at him again.

"Don't worry." He reached across the table to cover her hand with his, then pulled it back as if he thought better of it. The gesture lasted only an instant, making Cassidy not sure she'd imagined the shock that made her hand tingle and her heart race.

He got up. "It's late," he said, leaning down to peer through the blinds out into the night.

It was dark, the street empty except for an occasional car that passed.

"Why don't I help you close up and walk you to your car," he said.

"Really, that's not necessary—"

"I insist."

THE MOON WAS JUST COMING UP as they stepped outside the café. Cassidy breathed in the night air, too aware of Rourke's presence next to her.

It suddenly felt awkward between them. As if they'd been on a date and she wasn't sure if he was going to kiss her or not.

She fumbled for her car keys, dropped them. They both leaned down at the same time to pick them up. He got to them first and looked up at her, both still squatting down, so close she could smell his faint aftershave, feel the heat of his body warming the already warm night.

In the moonlight his face seemed softer, almost tender, and she was reminded of the boy who'd kissed her in the barn all those years ago.

At that moment, she couldn't have denied him anything.

He started to hand her the keys. His smile set her heart to pounding. So did the look in his eyes.

As their fingers met, he grasped her hand and pulled her toward him. His lips unerringly found hers, his mouth covering hers and, for a few fleeting seconds, she was lost in his kiss—just as she'd been in the barn.

And then as if history were destined to repeat itself, he pulled back. "Sorry." He pressed her keys into her hand before she could tell him he had nothing to be sorry about.

But she could see that, like her, he didn't want to break her heart again. He wasn't through with Blaze and they both knew it.

She nodded, unconsciously touching her tongue to her lower lip. It still tasted of him. Turning, she practically ran to her car.

She had opened the car door and started to get in, when she spotted the piece of folded paper stuck under the windshield.

Rourke must have been watching her because, in two long strides, he was at the car and plucking the note from under the wiper.

Cassidy watched him unfold the paper. He leaned toward the open car door to read it in the glow of the interior light.

She read over his shoulder, "Stay out of this if you know what's good for you or you will end up like Forrest."

The handwriting looked scribbled as if someone was purposely trying to disguise the penmanship.

Cassidy felt the blood rush from her head. She looked at Rourke. He didn't seem surprised and she knew at once why. "You've already gotten one of these, haven't you."

He looked from the note to her and nodded. "One. Pretty much the same message. Same handwriting."

He carefully folded the note and put it in his shirt pocket. "I'll take this note to Cash. Maybe you shouldn't go home tonight."

"I'll be fine."

"I don't like the idea of you staying at your place alone tonight."

What was he suggesting? Whatever it was, it was with obvious hesitation.

"Why don't you come with me?" he suggested, not sounding thrilled by the idea. "I'm staying out at the family cabin on the lake. There are two bedrooms but I don't use either—"

"Don't be ridiculous. It was just a silly note. Like you said, whoever is doing this isn't serious." There was no way she was going to his cabin. She'd promised herself she wouldn't fall for Rourke all over again. Ultimately, he would break her heart. Look how he kept defending Blaze. No matter what he said, he wasn't over her. And Cassidy wasn't going to let the two of them break her heart again.

"I'm quite capable of taking care of myself," she said. "Anyway," she added, glancing toward Antelope Development Corporation, "I have a pretty good idea who is behind this."

"You aren't suggesting that this is Blaze's doing?"

"No, I'm not suggesting. I'm telling you this has Blaze's style written all over it," Cassidy snapped. She felt her temper rise, angry at Blaze, at him. "You still have illusions about her." Cassidy shook her head and looked away, wanting to shake him. "Men." She got in and started her car.

He hadn't moved. He seemed unsure what to do next. He motioned for her to roll down her window.

She sighed and did, telling herself she was damned glad the kiss hadn't gone any further than it had. The man was an idiot. Why had she thought, when Rourke got out of prison, he might have matured, might finally see Blaze for what she was?

"Here's my cell-phone number in case you need me." He reached in and plucked the pen and pad from her uniform pocket and scribbled down his number. He handed the pen and pad back to her. "Be careful."

"Good night, Rourke," she said. "When you see Blaze, tell her to butt out of my life. I'll do anything I damned well please—including helping you." She drove off before he could say anything more. Probably because she had the feeling he was going to tell her he didn't want her help anymore.

When she glanced back in the rearview mirror, he was still standing there, looking after her. She thought of the kiss. It had been so tender, so… Her body demanded to know why she hadn't taken Rourke up on his offer.

Maybe he really was just offering you his bedroom. Or maybe he was offering you a night of pleasure beyond your wildest dreams. Good thing you aren't the kind of girl who is interested in a one-night stand.

Right.

"YOU SHOULDN'T HAVE touched it," Cash said as he bent over the piece of plain white paper and dusted it for prints.

"I wasn't thinking," Rourke said, and realized he'd been too upset both times he'd found the notes. This time, he'd been too shaken by the kiss.

Cash looked up at Rourke as if to say, *when are you ever thinking?*

He paced as he watched Cash dust the paper and check it against his own prints, which of course were on file. "Well?"

"It appears there is only one set of prints on the note, yours. The paper is white copier paper, the most common paper around."

"What about the handwriting?"

Cash shook his head. "Obviously disguised. Could have been written by a right-handed person using his left hand."

Rourke let out a sigh. "But it proves that I'm on to something."

Cash shook his head. "It proves someone doesn't want you bringing all this back up."

"Someone put a live rattler in a burlap bag behind my pickup seat my first day back in town," Rourke said.

Cash looked startled, then upset. "Dammit, Rourke, this is exactly what I was afraid of."

"Who do we know who sells rattlers?"

Cash chewed at his cheek for a moment. "Cecil Danvers for one."

"Easton Wells used to have a fondness for snakes," Rourke said.

"Have you seen him since you've been back?"

"No, but I'm thinking about paying him a visit."

Cash shook his head but saved his breath.

"Forrest had a wad of cash on him that night at the bar," Rourke said. He'd forgotten all about it until he'd talked to Kelly.

"It wasn't on him when he was found dead," Cash said.

"Exactly. And you didn't find it on me. So if he had

it when he left the bar but didn't when he was found, then the killer had to have taken it."

Cash nodded. "You're wondering where he got it and if anyone was a little richer after his murder."

"You know me so well," Rourke said with a grin.

"Sorry, bro. I have no idea what happened to the money. Nor did the state guys come up with anything. As for after his murder—" Cash was shaking his head "—there was a lot going on around here, but I don't remember anyone flashing any money around. Would have been a fool to."

Rourke knew he was just grasping at straws, but now that Cassidy was getting the notes, he felt pressure to find the killer before the threats possibly escalated.

Cash sighed and looked at his watch. "It's late. Why don't you let me talk to Cecil and Easton about the rattlesnake tomorrow?"

Rourke stood to leave. "No, I'd rather not let them know that I'm suspicious of them at this point. Easton used to be my best friend. We'll run into each other sooner or later." He didn't mention to Cash that he'd had him investigated and come up with something interesting. Cash would find out soon enough. The whole town would.

CASSIDY WAS SURPRISED by how exhausted she felt. She didn't even bother to turn on a light as she followed the path of moonlight streaming in the old farmhouse windows to her bedroom.

She couldn't believe how late it was. She shrugged out of her uniform, so tired she just tossed it aside. The blouse landed on the old trunk by the window and fell to the floor.

She stared at it for a moment, then tiredly went to pick it up. The letters. Now, more than ever, she didn't want Rourke finding out about them. She would build a fire in the fireplace and destroy them tonight.

She shoved aside the uniform blouse and opened the trunk. It was nearly full of the carefully addressed envelopes. She picked up one and stumbled back to sit on the edge of her bed. What had she been thinking?

She started to open the envelope. A thud outside the window startled her. She froze as she saw a shape move past, skulking along the side of the house. An instant later, she heard someone jiggle the back doorknob.

Her heart in her throat, she rose as if sleepwalking and inched her way toward the phone as she heard the lock on the back door break in the sharp splinter of wood.

She hurriedly dialed 9-1-1 and locked the bedroom door. She was surprised when Cash answered the phone instead of the night dispatcher.

"Cash, it's Cassidy. Someone is breaking into my house."

"Where are you, Cassidy?"

"In my bedroom at the house."

"Lock the door, push whatever you can against it and the windows, we're on our way."

We're? She could hear someone moving through the house. She hung up and got behind the large bureau and pushed with all her strength. For a moment, it didn't move. She could hear the intruder on the other side of the door, trying the lock.

The bureau slid with a lurch. She shoved it across the worn wooden floor to block the doorway, then looked toward the window. It was large and paned. Anyone who wanted to get to her could come through it without any trouble.

She grabbed the mattress off the bed and pulled it over to the window, then did the same with the box spring, standing it up, shutting out the moonlight.

She could hear the intruder trying to break down her bedroom door, angrily slamming against it again and again.

Then silence.

The silence terrified her. Where had he gone? She stood in the middle of the room, then rushed to the trunk and began to shove it toward the window. She stumbled over the mattress and almost fell, hitting her head on the box spring frame. Stars glittered in the darkness and she felt light-headed. She touched her forehead, her fingers coming away wet and sticky with her own blood.

The sound of shattering glass brought her out of her stupor. She pushed the trunk against the mattress and box spring, then she leaned against it, putting her weight into it, but she could tell it was a losing battle.

He was stronger than she was. She felt the mattress being forced into the room. She could hear his ragged breathing now, smell his sweat.

Then his hand found her hair. She let out a scream as he grabbed a handful of it and said her name.

Chapter Twelve

As the wail of the siren died off in Cassidy's yard, Rourke leaped from the patrol car and ran toward the house. He could hear Cash calling after him to wait.

The front door was locked. He ran around to the back.

The first thing he saw was the broken bedroom window and the crushed bush outside. From inside the house, he heard soft sobbing.

"Cassidy?" It was half call, half cry. He practically dove through the window.

She was slumped on the floor in the shaft of moonlight coming in through the window. She looked up at the sound of his voice. And the next thing he knew, he had her in his arms.

"He would have killed me if the siren hadn't scared him away," she whispered.

"Who?"

"Cecil Danvers."

Rourke held her in his arms, telling himself this was all his fault. He'd gotten her into this. She pressed her face into his chest for a moment, but when she heard Cash at the bedroom door, she stepped away, gathering a strength that he couldn't help but admire.

He shoved the bureau away from the door, unlocked the door and turned on the bedroom light. She stood, hugging herself, looking away from the window. There was a small cut on her forehead, but she was all right, he told himself. But he still wasn't leaving her alone again. He'd take her back to the cabin. He wouldn't let her out of his sight until Forrest's killer was caught.

He'd hesitated earlier because he'd been afraid of what people in town would think, her staying with a known criminal. Now he didn't give a damn. And while he was being honest with himself, he'd been afraid to take her to the cabin, unable to trust himself around her, and it had nothing to do with the fact that he hadn't been with anyone in eleven years. He was determined not to hurt her again.

"Are you all right?" Cash asked as he went to Cassidy.

Rourke stood back, watching the two of them for a moment. Did Cassidy care for his brother? It was obvious Cash cared for her. But not like a lover. More like a sister. Cash was still hung up on that woman from college.

She was telling Cash that it had been Cecil Danvers. Rourke started to turn away when he spotted something on the floor. A cream-colored envelope. What caught his attention was the name and address on the envelope. Rourke McCall #804376, 700 Conley Lake Road, Deer Lodge State Prison, Deer Lodge, Montana.

He leaned down and picked it up. His gaze shot up to the left-hand corner. The return address was Cassidy's.

He stared at it in confusion. He'd never received a

letter from Cassidy while he was in prison. Obviously she had never mailed it.

He glanced back toward her and saw the large old trunk she'd pushed up against the mattress and box spring. The lid on the trunk was partially open, an envelope the same color as the one in his hand was sticking out of the opening.

Another letter? He stepped to the trunk and lifted the lid. He caught his breath, never expecting to find the trunk full of letters. Dozens and dozens of them. All addressed to him. All never mailed.

He heard the soft gasp and turned to find Cassidy staring at him, one hand over her mouth, her eyes wide with a different kind of fear than what he'd witnessed earlier.

"I didn't mean to pry. It was lying on the floor."

She closed her eyes and nodded.

He stared at her. "What is this?"

Cash glanced at the trunk full of letters.

"I can explain," Cassidy said.

"I'll be outside if you need me," Cash said to her, then shot Rourke a warning look as he walked out of the bedroom. "I'll call in an APB on Cecil. He couldn't have gone far."

"What are these?" Rourke asked again after Cash was gone.

"Letters." Obviously. "I wrote you every Sunday for eleven years," she said, tears shining like jewels in her eyes.

He was flabbergasted. "Why didn't you mail them?"

She shook her head and looked away. "It's hard to explain." He waited. "I wanted to tell you how I felt. I guess I thought it would make a difference."

He couldn't believe this.

"I also wrote you about things that were going on in town, the weather, funny things that had happened at the café." She seemed to choke back a sob.

"Oh, Cassidy," he said, closing his eyes as he stepped to her and pulled her back into his arms. "I wish you'd mailed the letters."

He heard Cash come into the room, hesitate then clear his throat. Rourke let go of Cassidy and turned to face his brother. He didn't need to look far to see the disapproval on Cash's face.

"The highway patrol just picked up Cecil Danvers about a quarter mile from here in the ditch," Cash said, turning his attention to Cassidy. "He's drunk and bleeding from cuts on his hands. He admitted to coming after you, Cassidy. Any idea why?"

"I went out there this morning and asked him questions about his brother's murder," she said as if that explained it.

Cash shot Rourke a look. "This is your doing."

Rourke nodded and cursed himself. "I should never have gotten her involved."

"I *am* involved," she said.

Cash, to Rourke's surprise, nodded in agreement. "Well, Cecil is in jail so you won't have to worry about him. I doubt there is any chance he could make bail even if the judge allowed it. But you can't stay here. I was thinking I have that big, old house—"

"I'm taking her with me," Rourke said. "I'll see that nothing happens to her out at the cabin."

Cash motioned Rourke outside. "We'll just be a moment, Cassidy."

"What?" Rourke demanded, once they were out of earshot, although he knew what.

"Cassidy."

"Are you in love with her?"

"No, I just don't want to see her hurt."

"I don't, either," Rourke said. "I thought we already had this discussion?"

Cash sighed. "You know how you are with women."

"Actually, I don't. I was twenty-two when I went to prison."

"I would have thought you would hook up with Blaze as soon as you got out," Cash said.

Rourke nodded. "I would have thought so, too."

"Don't tell me she's not interested in you."

"Don't spread it around town, but it seems that my taste in women has changed." Rourke hadn't known how much. It was still hard for him to believe that Blaze no longer appealed to him and Cassidy did but not in the same way. With Blaze it was fun and games, nothing serious. With Cassidy…he felt shy, he thought with a laugh.

"What?" Cash demanded.

"I think I might finally be growing up. Don't look so surprised. I've got a ways to go."

Cash just shook his head. Back inside, Cash asked Cassidy what she wanted to do. Before she could answer, Rourke said, "She's coming with me." Then he added quietly to Cassidy, "Let me do this."

Cassidy seemed to hesitate, then nodded slowly.

Cash sighed. "I'll see about getting a sample of Cecil's handwriting when he sobers up so we can compare it to the threats you both received. I wouldn't be surprised if the handwriting matches."

Rourke glanced at Cassidy. She didn't believe that any more than he did. Cecil did things like break into a house with his bull head and no plan. He didn't write notes to scare someone. He came after the person with a sawed-off shotgun or his fists.

"I'll call Simon at the lumberyard and have him secure your house for you until he can put in a new window," Cash said to Cassidy.

"Thank you, Cash."

He nodded, looking worried. "We don't know yet if Cecil killed Forrest. So, be careful, okay?"

"I wouldn't be surprised if he breaks down and confesses," Rourke said. "It would definitely explain why he was acting odder than usual the night Forrest was murdered." He told Cash about what Cassidy had learned.

"Cecil caught a ride with Blaze?" Cash said. "Then he was there during the fight and even for a while afterward. He could have known where Forrest was headed, could have gone up there easily enough after he got a ride home—or even been waiting for Forrest when Forrest got there."

"Looks like Cecil just pushed himself to the head of the suspect list," Rourke said.

CASSIDY HAD HEARD about the McCall cabin on the lake but she'd never been there before.

"It's pretty rustic," Rourke said as he parked behind it. He sounded as if he was worried she wouldn't like the place. Was it possible she was the first woman he'd ever brought here?

The inside of the cabin was small but neat, everything in miniature.

"This is your bedroom," he said pointing into a room with four bunk beds and a large chest of drawers. "It's the big one," he said with a laugh. "This is the master bedroom."

She walked the few feet to the next room and peeked inside. He was right. It was just large enough for a double bed. "This must have been your parents' room."

"Way back when. It's funny but Asa never slept in there after her alleged death. He always opted for the porch cot and let us boys fight over who got the big bed." He smiled. "I thought it was because he missed my mother and couldn't deal with her death. Now I'm not so sure."

"Couldn't it just be that he loved her and the room reminded him of everything he'd given up?"

Rourke looked down at her for a long moment. She practically squirmed under his intensity.

"Maybe you're right," he said quietly. "Want to see the rest of the cabin?" He led her through a small living-room area with rustic furniture and a bookshelf filled with classics and board games. No TV.

"It's wonderful," she cried, then blushed.

"I'm glad you like it," he said. "I don't have much in the fridge, but I do have beer," he said as he stepped into the kitchen. He turned and held up a bottle of beer.

To her surprise, she nodded, not wanting to call it a night yet. Earlier she'd been so exhausted, she thought as she walked to the wide expanse of windows that looked out on a screened-in porch and, beyond that, the lake.

The moon had scaled the mountains and now hovered over the lake, huge and buttery-yellow, the water shimmering like liquid gold.

"Let's go out on the porch," Rourke suggested as he uncapped her beer and handed it to her.

On the screened-in porch, he pushed open the door and she joined him as he sat on the top step and looked out at the lake. Only a slight breeze whispered in the pines above the shoreline. The night was still, warm and scented with the last days of summer.

"Pretty, isn't it," he said, beside her, and took a sip of his beer.

"Breathtaking."

"See that spot right over there," he asked, pointing to an outcrop of rocks at the edge of the water. "I was fishing there once when I was about six and I hooked into a huge bass. I'm telling you, it was the biggest fish I've ever seen in my life. Cash and J.T. were cheering me on, although it was clear they thought I couldn't possibly land it." He was lost in memory for a few moments.

"Did you?"

"Hmm? Oh, I landed it all right. J.T. thought it was a state record. He'd run to get something to weigh it. Cash was yelling at Dad that we were going to have bass for dinner."

She was watching him, recognized his wry expression and knew. "You let it go."

His smile broadened as he looked over at her. "Yeah. I never heard the end of it." Their eyes met, making her heart compress. Cassidy could feel the heat, almost see the sparks flying back and forth between them.

Rourke glanced away and took a drink of his beer.

Since the day he'd come back, he had talked to her about nothing but Forrest's murder. Tonight he wasn't that embittered man who'd come out of prison seeking vengeance. Nor was he the wild boy. He was someone in between, someone who made her feel warm and safe and alive sitting next to him. She wished this night would never end.

They finished their beers in a companionable silence, but she was never more aware of a man as she was Rourke. As he shifted to point out one thing or another, their thighs would brush and heat would spread through her. Her flesh felt on fire. She hugged herself, suddenly wondering if she'd made a mistake coming out here with him.

She wanted him to kiss her. No, not just kiss her. She wanted him to make love to her. To hell with tomorrow. She would have given anything to lie in Rourke's arms tonight.

Her heart pounded a little harder at just the thought of waking up tomorrow in his arms. Uh-huh. And having him tell you that last night was a mistake? And it would be a mistake. She knew that. Not that it made it any easier to push the fantasy away and rise to her feet. "I should get some sleep."

He rose with her. "Cassidy, I'm sorry I got you involved in this."

She shook her head. "I was already involved and I volunteered to help you."

"With a little arm-twisting," he said.

"I can take a lot of arm-twisting if I don't want to do something," she said and turned to go inside but he caught her hand—and just as quickly let go of it.

"Thanks," he said, and nodded as if that was all he wanted to say. Or do. But his gaze went to her lips. Her pulse quickened and she knew all she had to do was lean a little toward him, her face lifted to his and he would kiss her.

"CASSIDY." He hadn't even realized he'd said her name. Nor that he'd moved to her. He looked into her face and wondered how he could not have noticed her eleven years ago. She was so appealing, from her understated beauty and warm brown eyes to her golden mane of hair that tumbled around her shoulders and the soft cadence of her voice.

But it was the tenderness he saw in her eyes, the shyness that tugged at his cynical heart and made him feel weak in the knees around her.

There was something about her that made it easy to talk to her, easy to be around her. There was an intelligence and a determination that exemplified why she had done so well with the Longhorn Café. Not to mention, a kindness, a goodness that seemed to radiate from her face.

He admired the hell out of her.

But what he was feeling now went beyond admiration.

She was frowning at him, her head cocked a little to one side, her eyes bright as sunlight.

Kissing her right then was as natural as breathing. And yet he hesitated. He didn't want to mess this up, and he feared kissing her might ruin something good. He liked her, felt they were becoming friends. He didn't want to lose that.

But he only hesitated a moment. His desire to kiss her overpowered everything. Throwing caution to the wind, he leaned toward her.

She didn't pull back. Her eyes widened, her lips parted. He dropped his mouth to hers. A soft, gentle brush of a kiss.

She seemed to hold her breath, eyes wide. Then she giggled. "Sorry," she said.

He shook his head, pulling back to smile at her.

"I'm a little—" she hiccuped "—nervous."

His smile broadened. She had the hiccups? "Can I get you a glass of water?"

She nodded and hiccuped again, her face reddening. "Oh, I am so embarrassed," he heard her say under her breath, which only made him smile more as he went into the kitchen and got her a glass of water.

"Here," he said, when he came back out.

She took the water and gulped it down, holding her head back. "I get the hiccups when I'm...nervous."

"I'm sorry I make you nervous."

She swallowed the rest of the water, then they both waited to see if the water did the trick.

She laughed in relief and he laughed with her, but as their laughter died, the atmosphere between them seemed to change as if the molecules themselves had become charged with electricity.

"I should..." She made a motion toward her bedroom.

He looked at her and smiled. He wasn't going to mess this up. No way. "Good night."

She nodded, seeming disappointed. Not half as much as he was. But the more he was around Cassidy, the more he liked her. The more he was determined not to hurt her.

As the door closed, he stood on the steps and silently

cursed himself. So much for his pledge not to get too close to her. He couldn't believe he'd kissed her. If she hadn't gotten the hiccups...

He smiled to himself remembering. He liked Cassidy. She seemed to bring out something good and strong in him, something he liked.

He let out a long breath and stared up at the moon. It felt as if he'd never seen it before, as if his life really was beginning all over again. How about that?

He went onto the porch and sprawled on the cot, the moonlight filtering in through the screens. For the first time in a long while, he felt at peace.

Chapter Thirteen

The next morning Rourke woke to the sound of a vehicle coming up the road. He rose, surprised how well he'd slept last night.

Cassidy's bedroom door was closed as he padded to the back porch. He suspected it would be Cash coming out to check on Cassidy.

But as the vehicle drew closer, he saw that it wasn't the sheriff's patrol car but one of the green Suburbans from Antelope Development Corporation. Easton? He'd been expecting a visit from him. The Suburban pulled up, morning sun glaring off the windshield. The door opened.

He groaned as Blaze stepped out. What did she want?

"You're a hard man to find," Blaze said, coming to a halt at the bottom of the steps. She looked up at him as if waiting for an invitation.

"What can I do for you, Blaze?" he asked, leaning against the railing, not inviting her inside.

She seemed to take in his rumpled T-shirt and jeans, his bare feet.

"I have something important I wanted to tell you,"

she said. "About the night Forrest was killed." She looked pointedly at the door to the cabin. "Well?"

He knew it was probably just a ruse. "Okay." He motioned her in, leaving the door open as he walked back into the cabin to the kitchen where he started a pot of coffee.

When he turned, she was right behind him. He swore under his breath, angry with himself for the shot of desire that bulleted through him at just the familiar scent of her perfume. It brought back a wave of sexual memories that reminded him how long it had been.

With Blaze it would be so easy. Hadn't he promised himself that the next time he got a chance, he'd sleep with her? Well, this wasn't that chance given that Cassidy was in the next room. But the idea definitely had its appeal.

He'd noticed the last couple of days that his libido was starting to resurface. He didn't trust himself with Cassidy. Maybe if he took Blaze up on her offer, it would make it easier to be around Cassidy.

He took a breath. "There was something you wanted to tell me?"

"A cup of coffee would be nice."

"It's brewing."

She stepped closer. "It's been a long time," she whispered. "I never forgot you, Rourke." And then her mouth was on his.

He closed his eyes, lost in the kiss, in the familiar. But then he opened his eyes and saw Blaze and pulled back.

She blinked in surprise. "What?"

He shook his head. He could no more explain it than speak at the moment. Blaze was a sexy woman and the offer was clear, but he wasn't interested even if Cassidy hadn't been in the next room. It surprised him more than it did even her.

He looked past Blaze and saw Cassidy and knew she'd witnessed the kiss. Damn. She was wearing his robe. She met his eyes for only an instant, then hurried into the bathroom, closing the door silently behind her.

Blaze hadn't seen Cassidy or heard her pad quietly to the bathroom. "Come on, stop playing hard to get. You know you want me."

"Sorry, Blaze, but I don't want you."

She glared at him with a mixture of anger and contempt in her eyes. "This is a one-time offer, Rourke."

Surprisingly he was glad to hear that. He heard the shower come on. Blaze didn't seem to notice. "What is it you wanted to tell me about Forrest's murder?"

She shook her head and he figured it would be a cold day in hell before he ever found out.

"Unless you were lying about having something you wanted to tell me," he added.

She bristled at that. "Yvonne Ames." She practically spit the words at him. "She's the woman who was meeting Forrest the night he was murdered."

He couldn't have been more surprised. "How do you know that?"

"She told me. In so many words. She came by to see me because she thought I'd be seeing you." Blaze glared at him. "She was afraid you were going to find out. She asked me if you'd said anything about her since you'd been back. She said she sent you letters and cookies at prison. I knew she was lying."

Yvonne had never been overly bright. Going to Blaze was one of her dumber moves. She was lucky Blaze hadn't strangled her on the spot. Blaze had to be beside herself at even the thought that Forrest was seeing her and Yvonne Ames. It definitely put Blaze in a category she didn't want to be.

"What's so funny?" she demanded.

He shook his head. The shower stopped. "It must have ticked you off royally to find out Forrest was running around with you and Yvonne."

"I didn't see a ring on my finger," she snapped. "I could date anyone I wanted."

"Seems Forrest felt the same way."

She whipped around angrily and he thought she was going to stomp out right then. Instead her expression softened. "Rourke, don't do this." She pressed her palms against his T-shirt and gave him the come-hither look that used to draw him to her like a bear to honey. *Now or never,* her look said.

Never, he thought, surprising the hell out of him.

"I know you're angry with me," she purred. "But if you could just forgive me, you and I could—"

"Blaze, that's not it. I'm not angry. I'm just not…interested."

She reared back as if he'd slapped her.

Just then, Cassidy came out of the bathroom, wearing his robe, her hair wet and clinging to her flushed skin.

Blaze turned and let out a curse before swinging back around to face him, her face hardening to stone. "You just made the biggest mistake of your life." Then she stormed out, slamming the door behind her.

Cassidy was also giving him a look. "You have lipstick on your cheek," she said, and walked down the hall to the bedroom, closing the door behind her.

BLAZE DROVE like a demon back into Antelope Flats. Rourke didn't know who he was dealing with. She'd show him. He would rue this day, so help her, God.

She pushed open the door to ADC ignoring the receptionist's cheery "good morning," and stormed into the office, dropping her purse and keys onto her desk before turning, surprised to see Easton at his desk.

He looked so good this morning she almost poured her heart out to him. "Something wrong?" he asked.

Everything was wrong. Nothing was going the way she'd planned it. And worst of all, Cassidy was with Rourke. She felt tears flood her eyes and realized what was killing her. She didn't care about Rourke, she never had. She just didn't want Cassidy to have him. And she wanted Easton to be so jealous that he'd break down and finally ask her to marry him.

As she stared at Easton, she realized what a fool she'd been. "Oh, Easton." She threw herself into his lap.

He caught her, obviously surprised by her outburst. "Let me guess. Rourke."

"This isn't about Rourke. It never was. You're the only man I love." She wiped her eyes and he reached into his pocket for his handkerchief. He handed it to her. It was true, she realized with a start. She loved him.

Easton laughed. "Blaze, you really are something. Love? You might want to marry me. Or at least think you do right now."

She blinked. "I'm serious. The past few days have made me realize just what you mean to me."

His eyes narrowed and he stood, forcing her off his lap. He walked around the end of his desk, putting distance between them. "What's going on with Rourke?"

"Nothing!"

"So that's it."

"No, I don't care about Rourke. He didn't even come back the same man I knew."

"What a surprise after eleven years in prison."

Blaze stared at him. Easton had never been this snide to her, never this cold. A chasm of fear opened up inside her. "East, I never wanted Rourke. I just wanted to make you jealous, make you realize that you couldn't live without me."

He let out a startled laugh. "Did I just hear the truth come out of your mouth? This is a first."

She lowered herself into the chair he'd vacated feeling suddenly too weak to stand. She dropped her head, crying in front of him, no longer worrying about what it would do to her makeup. "You have to believe me. I love you."

"Really, Blaze? What if I had no money?"

She looked up at him in surprise.

"What if I lost everything? What if we had to live the rest of our lives in that dinky apartment of yours? Would you still love me then, Blaze?"

She was trying to imagine why he would lose everything.

"That's what I thought." He strode to the door, his face hard with anger. "I can see the answer in your face. Don't even try to deny it."

"No," she said, stumbling out of the chair. "I...would love you. I would. I do. Easton, please."

But it was too late. He stormed out, slamming the door, leaving her alone. She dropped back into the chair and buried her face in her hands.

Why would Easton lose everything? It must have something to do with Rourke. That would explain why Easton had been acting strangely lately. He and Rourke had been best friends. Was it possible Easton really did have something to do with Forrest's murder?

She felt strangely protective of Easton as she forced the sobs to recede, dried her eyes and picked up her purse. She would help Easton any way she could.

ROURKE WAS UNUSUALLY QUIET on the drive into town. Cassidy suspected it was because he was regretting having turned down Blaze.

"I'm sorry I complicated things for you this morning at the cabin," she said, glancing over at him.

"I assume you heard everything."

"Not *everything*," she said, trying to sound indignant. "I've already told you. I could care less about you and Blaze. That was all in the past." She could feel his eyes on her. Did he suspect she let the shower run while she listened with her ear to the door and then took a speedy shower? "Blaze is obviously still interested in you. I'm surprised you don't take her up on her…offers."

Rourke laughed. "Me, too. Did you hear what she told me?"

Cassidy couldn't remember if she was supposed to be in the shower during that discussion. "What was that?"

He eyed her suspiciously. "That she believes Yvonne Ames was meeting Forrest the night he was murdered."

Cassidy widened her eyes at him.

He smiled and shook his head. "I thought maybe you and I could stop by and talk to Yvonne. She might be more likely to talk to a woman about it than me." He glanced over at her again. "What do you say?"

"I need to get changed and go to work." What she needed to do was distance herself from Rourke. It was just a matter of time before Blaze got to him and he gave in to her. Cassidy had to remember that.

"Sure." He sounded disappointed that she wasn't coming with him.

True to his word, Cash had seen that a large sheet of plywood had been placed where the window had been in her bedroom. The house looked fine. Rourke offered to check the outside while she changed.

She thought about the kiss last night at the cabin. Hurriedly brushed it from her thoughts as she heard Rourke come back into the house. Blaze would do whatever it took to get back at him.

"Mind if I use your phone to call Yvonne?" he called.

"Help yourself." She heard him dial.

"No answer. What do you say to a change of plans?" She could hear him just outside the bedroom door. She didn't trust her voice. "I was thinking we could go for a horseback ride this morning. I can get Martha to make us a brunch basket."

She opened the bedroom door and looked at him. Was he serious? Hadn't she just said she had to go to work? "I own a business, Rourke—"

"I know. I was just hoping you could take off the morning so we could ride up Wild Horse Gulch. The back way," he said.

She stared at him. "You think the killer went by horseback?"

"It crossed my mind after what Cecil told you," he said. "Four landowners have the property in that area, my family, Blaze's father, the Forest Service and Mason VanHorn. I didn't see anyone else on the road that night or any other car parked at the end of the road."

"Cecil is in jail," she said. "You still want to keep investigating?"

"I want to spend the day with you and I know this spot that is perfect for a picnic. Say you'll come with me."

She thought about him and Blaze and what she'd witnessed this morning and warned herself not to get involved with Rourke McCall. He wasn't over Blaze. No matter what he said. "I really need to get to work."

"Okay, I don't think Cecil killed his brother. The truth is I'm still investigating and you promised to help me," he said, and grinned.

"You're that determined to get me to go with you?"

"Yes."

"Did you mean it about Cecil?" she asked.

He shrugged, still grinning. "Maybe."

"This isn't about keeping an eye on me, is it?"

He pretended to be offended. "Would I be that transparent?"

She knew she shouldn't but in truth, she wanted to go riding with him. She felt herself weaken. "I'll call the café and see if they can get by without me for a few hours."

He grinned from ear to ear. "Thanks. I really appreciate this."

WHEN SHE CALLED the Longhorn, Arthur said he and Ellie could handle it. She promised to be in later to help with the dinner rolls and bread. Then she changed into jeans, a snap-button Western shirt, boots and her jean jacket and cowboy hat.

When she came back into the living room, Rourke looked up, his gaze caressing her as it moved slowly over her body, lighting on her face.

"What?" she asked, feeling embarrassed by his scrutiny. She turned to peer into the hall mirror.

He laughed and shook his head, his smile broadening. "I was just admiring your face. It's a wonderful face. You don't even need makeup."

"Thank you. I think."

"Come on, I can't wait to get back in the saddle," he said, and winked at her.

She walked past him to the pickup and could almost feel him watching her behind. She hid a smile as he hurried to open her door. This felt like a date. She warned herself to be careful.

She hadn't been out to the McCall Ranch in years. She was glad to see that it hadn't changed. Rourke gazed out at the landscape as if he couldn't get enough of it.

"When this is all over," he said, "I think I'm going to help my brothers with the ranch." He glanced over at her. "You don't seem surprised."

"I always knew you would," she said, and looked away from him. "You love the ranch. It's a part of you."

Rourke laughed. "Maybe you know me better than I know myself."

Maybe, she thought.

He parked the pickup and they walked down the hillside to the barn. The same barn where Rourke had kissed her when she was thirteen. She followed him inside, fighting the memories.

The day Rourke had kissed her she'd come out to the ranch with her father to deliver a load of oats to Asa. While they unloaded it, Asa suggested J.T. show her the horses. But Rourke had volunteered.

She had thought her heart might stop. It had been the happiest moment of her life as he'd led her out to the horse barn.

Inside, she had watched him with the horses, heartened to see that he obviously loved horses as much as she did. She'd thought then that she and Rourke were perfect for each other.

"Would you like to ride sometime?" he'd asked just when she thought the day couldn't get any better.

She nodded, unable to trust her voice, and he'd smiled at her in his sweet, tender way, and that's when she'd realized he was going to kiss her.

Her breath had caught in her throat as he'd cupped her cheek and dropped his head. And then his lips were on hers, sealing her fate. That fate being unrequited love.

"You all right?" Rourke asked now.

She blinked, focusing on the present. From the look on his face, he'd been studying her.

"I thought you could use one of my sister's saddles and ride Sunshine," he said still eyeing her closely.

She took the saddle he handed her and nodded, unable to trust her voice just as she had so many years ago. That kiss had started her heart along this path. And the kisses since then had only made her more sure that she'd fallen in love with a man who might never really see her for one reason or another.

She saddled Sunshine, practically hiding behind the horse. Even if he'd forgotten about her kiss, he had to have seen her feelings so clearly on her face.

They led the horses out of the barn, Cassidy intently aware of Rourke beside her, glad when they'd left the cool darkness of the barn, so full of memory and young-girl hopes, for the warmth and clarity of the morning sunshine.

The air was still cool from the night before as they rode across to the foothills, then climbed up over the mountains to drop into the gulch.

"I didn't realize how much I've missed this," Rourke said, breathing in deeply. He glanced over at her as if she was the one person he knew understood.

The McCall ranch ran over several drainages ending in a stretch of Forest Service land that connected with Wild Horse Gulch. Beyond the gulch was a section of Logan land that Blaze's father owned. The rest was VanHorn land. VanHorn had been buying up everything he could get his hands on ever since he'd discovered there was coal-bed methane.

They stopped on a mountain ridge overlooking the gulch. Rourke carried the brunch basket Martha had made to a cluster of magnificent ponderosa pines and spread out the blanket on the dried pine needles. A breeze whispered softly in the boughs overhead.

They ate, talking about everything under the sun except for murder and Blaze Logan. He seemed to like listening to her and encouraged her to talk about herself, something she felt awkward doing.

"I never forgot our kiss in the barn," he said after a while. "I'm sorry I never followed up on it."

She felt her face flush as he reached over to brush her hair back from her cheek.

He stared into her face, her lovely face. Her scent mixed with the scents of the land he'd always loved and he felt weak with a need to kiss her again.

Her mouth was wide and generous, her lips full and heart-shaped. And when she smiled—

She was smiling at him now, her head cocked a little to one side, her eyes bright as sunlight.

He'd known he would kiss her again. It was all he'd thought about since last night. He leaned toward her, brushing his lips over that wonderful mouth.

He pulled back to look into her eyes. She was beautiful! The thought hit him like a brick. It wasn't just her face or her eyes or her smile. Everything about this woman was like sunshine.

He'd never wanted anything more than to be with her right now. Not even his freedom from prison. He leaned toward her again, cupping her cheek with his palm. With Cassidy, he felt like he'd really come home.

"Cassidy." It was as if all of his feelings were wrapped up in that one word.

Her eyes darkened with desire and her lips parted as he dropped his mouth to hers. He pressed her back into the blanket, the scent of pine and her filling his nostrils.

He heard her catch her breath and thought he could hear her heart pounding and realized it was his own. He pulled back. "Cassidy?"

The look in her eyes was answer enough. He kissed her again, deepening the kiss, burying his hand in her hair.

His pulse was pounding so hard he didn't hear the first shot.

But the horses did. They started, rearing back from where he'd tied them a few yards away, their heads coming up in startled surprise.

The second shot came on the heels of the first, this one closer. Rourke threw himself on top of Cassidy, rolling them both across the blanket to the cover of the thick trunks of the pines. The shots had come from the gulch. He heard an engine crank up.

"Stay here," he ordered Cassidy as he scrambled out from the pines and ran to the edge of the ridge. A green Suburban with ADC on the side disappeared in a cloud of dust over a rise and was gone.

But in the sunlight, he spotted one gold spent casing lying in the dust not far from where he'd found Forrest in his pickup.

"It was just another warning," Cassidy said beside him. "Just like the notes."

"Except Cecil is in jail."

She nodded. "This wasn't Cecil."

"No," he said. "I caught a glimpse of the vehicle as it was racing away. It was one of the green Antelope Development Corporation Suburbans."

"Blaze," Cassidy said on a breath.

He didn't bother to argue it could have easily been Easton. He dropped down, carefully retrieving the casing from the dust. "Let's get back to town," he said, looking up to see Cassidy watching him closely. "I'll take you to the café where you'll be safe, then I'll drop off the shell with Cash."

As CASSIDY WALKED in the back door of the Longhorn Café a couple of customers called to her. Les Thurman from the Mello Dee was sitting at the counter. He gave her a nod. Past him, she saw Holt VanHorn. He looked like he was waiting for someone. Cassidy glimpsed a pickup outside the café. There was a person sitting in it. Cecil? Was it possible he'd somehow made bail?

Cassidy was so angry with Blaze, it was all she could do not to storm over there and accost her. Blaze seemed hell-bent on keeping Cassidy away from Rourke and had since Cassidy was thirteen.

The worst part was, Blaze's plan was working. Cassidy wondered if Rourke regretted that they hadn't made love under the pines as much as she did.

He hadn't said much on the way back to town, insisting he follow her from her house to the café to make sure she was safe. She wanted desperately to know what he was thinking, then decided it might be best not to.

The phone rang. Ellie picked it up before Cassidy had a chance and, turning, covered the receiver to say, "It's Yvonne Ames."

Cassidy couldn't imagine why Yvonne would be calling her. She stepped into her office to take it, leaving the door open. "Hello?" Silence. "Hello?"

"Cassidy?" Yvonne sounded upset. "I have to talk to you." She sounded as if she'd been crying. "I heard you were helping Rourke look for Forrest's murderer?"

"Yes. What's wrong, Yvonne?"

"I know I should have come forward eleven years ago, but I couldn't. You have to understand. If my father had found out that I was meeting Forrest—and then after what happened, I couldn't tell anyone."

"You saw Forrest that night up Wild Horse Gulch?" Cassidy said, and realized her voice had probably carried out into the café. She hurriedly closed the office door. "Yvonne, did you see the killer?"

Yvonne was crying, sobbing, her words indistinguishable. Then, "I have to blow my nose." She dropped the phone.

Cassidy waited impatiently. Was it possible Yvonne really had been the woman Forrest was meeting and not Blaze? And had Yvonne seen something?

"Sorry," Yvonne said, finally picking up the phone again.

"You were there that night?

"I didn't see the killer," she said.

Cassidy's hopes sank.

"When I got there, Forrest was still alive. The killer had just left. I don't think he saw me. He took off on a horse."

Just as Rourke had suspected.

"Forrest had something in his hand. It was a St. Christopher medal on a chain. It had blood all over it."

"Forrest's?" Cassidy asked.

"No. The chain was broken. I think Forrest must have reached for his killer and grabbed the chain."

"Yvonne, you've had something of the killer's all these years and you've never said anything?"

"I couldn't." She began to cry again. "I didn't know who killed Forrest. It's just a medal. If I told the police all it would do was let the killer know I was there that night. I didn't see anything, but he wouldn't know that for sure. He'd kill me, too."

The medal might have cleared Rourke, might have

helped find the real killer eleven years ago. "Yvonne, why are you telling me this now?"

"I'm afraid. I think he's found out somehow that I was the one there that night."

"Where is this medal?" Cassidy heard a sound in the background at Yvonne's. "What was that?"

"Someone is at the door again."

Again? "Don't answer it," Cassidy cried, suddenly afraid.

Yvonne choked back a sob just before she dropped the phone again. Cassidy heard a voice. It sounded like Blaze's stepbrother Gavin.

"Yvonne? Yvonne?!" Cassidy fumbled her cell phone out of her purse and dialed 9-1-1, keeping both phones to her ear. She could hear nothing on Yvonne's end.

The dispatcher said Cash was unavailable at the moment.

"Tell him to go to Yvonne Ames's house," Cassidy said. "I'll meet him there. It's urgent."

"Yvonne? Yvonne?" Cassidy listened for a few moments, thought she heard a scuffing sound but Yvonne didn't come back on the line. She left the phone off the hook, grabbed her purse and left. What had she done with Rourke's cell phone number? She'd left it on the table by the door at her house.

She couldn't wait for Cash. Maybe the person at the door had been a beauty supply salesman. Cassidy told herself she was overreacting. But she thought she'd heard Gavin's voice. What if someone *had* found out that Yvonne was the woman meeting Forrest up Wild Horse Gulch that night and had kept it to herself all these years?

What was Cassidy thinking? If Blaze knew, then the whole town could know by now—let alone her stepbrother Gavin.

"WHERE HAVE YOU BEEN?" Easton asked as Blaze came into the office. She looked scared and upset and her clothing was a mess, dusty and dirty.

She seemed surprised to see him, and at the same time, relieved. "I have to tell you something."

He nodded. "And I have something to tell you, too, something I think you already know, or at least suspect. I'm in trouble. I did some creative bookkeeping when I first started this business. Rourke hired a private investigator and now the auditors are coming to go over my books—the real books. I'll probably be going to jail for a while." He waited for her to say something.

She stared at him, then began to laugh and cry at the same time,

"You're taking it better than I expected," he said. "I figured you were only interested in marrying me for my money and once you realized there was no money…"

"I thought you killed Forrest," she managed to get out between sobs.

"Oh, Blaze," he said, and opened his arms as he moved to her.

She stepped into his arms. "I did something really stupid eleven years ago and again today, East."

"Did you kill anyone?" he asked, holding his breath.

She shook her head. "But I lied about where I was the night Forrest died. I tried to follow Forrest. I thought he was meeting someone else. I lost him, but Cecil knew because I gave him a ride as far as my dad's ranch."

"Has Cecil been blackmailing you?" Easton asked, wondering how Cecil had made bail. He'd just seen him on the street outside.

"Cecil isn't that smart," she said.

Easton watched as Rourke's pickup pulled up out front, then the sheriff's patrol car. The two men got out and looked into the Suburban Blaze had just returned in. His heart caught in his throat. He hadn't realized how much he didn't want to lose Blaze until that moment. "Blaze, I think you'd better tell me what you did today."

THE SUN WAS HOT coming in the car windows as Cassidy drove to the outskirts of town. Yvonne lived in a small house that she'd bought after beauty school. The front of the building housed her beauty shop, Hair For You.

As Cassidy drove up, she saw that the Closed sign was still in the window of the shop. She climbed out of her car and went to pound on the door. Locked. Peering in the window, she could see the place was empty, the door that went into the apartment part of the house closed.

The lot next door was waist-high weeds. On the other side, there was a flower shop that had gone broke, the windows soaped, a For Lease sign out front.

Across the street were more empty lots and several old houses that were in the process of being torn down for a minimall that she'd heard Easton was building.

Cassidy hurried down the narrow sidewalk along the side of the house. Yvonne's small blue car was parked at the back next to a shed.

Grasshoppers rustled in the tall weeds, the air back

here hot and rank. She caught a whiff of the garbage cans along the dirt alley as she stepped up to the back door and knocked. No answer.

"Yvonne!" she called, and pounded on the door. Through a crack in the curtain, she peered into the house but could see nothing beyond the small kitchen and breakfast nook.

She tried the knob. To her surprise and concern, the door swung open. She stood for a moment, wishing Rourke was here with her. Wishing she heard the sound of Cash's siren.

Silence. Except for the chirp of the grasshoppers.

She peered in and saw two dirty plates on a small breakfast-nook table, a half-eaten slice of bacon sitting in the congealed egg yolk on one. Yvonne had had company.

"Yvonne?" She stepped in and had to stifle a gasp. The house had been ransacked, everything pulled out of drawers and cabinets.

She stood looking at the mess. Wait for Cash. A noise came from upstairs. Like the scuff of a shoe on the wood floor, the same sound she'd heard earlier on the phone. "Yvonne?"

The living room was also ransacked. A floorboard creaked overhead. Cassidy looked up the narrow stairway against the wall. She could see nothing at the top of the stairs but shadowy darkness.

Wait for Cash, her instincts told her. Don't go up there alone.

But as she started up the steps, Cassidy knew she had to go up. She had to see if Yvonne was up there, maybe hurt. Another creak of a floorboard.

"Yvonne?" No answer. Just the old house creaking like old houses tended to do.

Cassidy ascended the steps coming out on a short dark landing with three doors, two closed, one partially open. She started toward the door that was open a crack.

"Yvonne?" she called as she pushed the door slowly open.

"THERE'S A .22 RIFLE under the back seat of this one and the engine is still warm," Rourke said as he and Cash moved along the side of the green ADC Suburbans.

"I'll go down the street and get a warrant from Judge McGowan," Cash said. "You think you can keep Blaze and Easton from leaving until I get back?"

Rourke just laughed and headed for the front door of ADC. He tipped his hat to the receptionist, not bothering to stop, going straight to Blaze and Easton's office. He wasn't in the mood to wait for anything. Cash had told him that Cecil Danvers had made bail. The good news was that there was a decent print on the casing they'd found up Wild Horse Gulch.

Rourke still couldn't believe either Blaze or Easton had taken a potshot at him and Cassidy. He knew the reason he was so angry was because of what the shooter had interrupted. He was kicking himself for taking Cassidy up there and yet, at the same time, he couldn't remember a morning ride he'd enjoyed more. He knew it was probably for the best that he and Cassidy hadn't made love up there. But it didn't help his mood any.

He'd followed Cassidy to the café, making sure she was safe before going by the sheriff's office. Cassidy hadn't said much on the way to her place to change her clothing or on the trip into town. He couldn't wait to see her again. He had to know what she was thinking, what she was feeling.

Easton and Blaze both turned in surprise as the door opened and he walked in.

"Rourke," Blaze said. She'd obviously been crying. She shot a glance at Easton.

He had stepped forward as if to protect her. It surprised Rourke. He'd just assumed Easton didn't care that much about Blaze since he hadn't married her.

"Which one of you just got back from Wild Horse Gulch?" Rourke asked, unable to miss the look Easton shot Blaze.

"I did," he said, and Blaze couldn't seem to hide her surprise. "What's the problem?"

"Someone driving a green ADC Suburban just took a couple potshots at Cassidy and me."

Easton was shaking his head. "Can you prove that?" He stole a glance at Blaze, obvious worry on his face. "I'm sure this is just a misunderstanding."

Rourke smiled. "Just like Forrest's murder?"

"I didn't have anything to do with that," Easton said. "Look, Rourke, could we talk about this?" He shot a glance at Blaze, who'd sat back down behind her desk. She looked scared.

"Why don't we step outside," Rourke said.

Easton raised a brow. "Okay."

As they left the office, Rourke told the receptionist to make sure Blaze didn't leave.

"I'm sorry I didn't make an effort to come see you in prison," Easton said. "I feel bad about that."

Rourke nodded. "But you started dating Blaze the

second I left town, so that probably would have made it awkward during your visit."

"Well, you're here now. There's nothing keeping you from taking Blaze back."

Rourke smiled at that. "Actually there is, but it's not you. I'm interested in someone else." The admission surprised him. "Blaze and I were never serious about each other any way. At least Blaze wasn't."

Easton raised a brow and glanced toward the office as if things were clearer now. "Blaze and I are going to be getting married."

Rourke couldn't hide his surprise. "Why now? It's been eleven years."

"I guess I wanted to be sure she was over you. She loves me and I love her." He seemed to challenge Rourke to say otherwise.

Something passed between them, a remnant of the friendship they'd once shared.

"Congratulations," Rourke said, and meant it. "Too bad one of you will be behind bars. I know Blaze took the shots at us, not you. You're willing to go to prison for her?"

Easton let out a soft, amused chuckle. It reminded Rourke of all the good times they'd shared. Gone, just like the past eleven years. But not forgotten. "I think we both know that I'm headed in that direction already and, like I said, we love each other. We're two of a kind, as it turns out."

Cash came up the street with the warrant. Easton took it and nodded, watching while Cash searched the Suburban and found the rifle.

"I'm the person you're looking for," Easton lied. "I did it."

"Why?" Cash asked. He could have meant why did you do it. But Rourke suspected, like him, Cash knew Easton was covering for Blaze.

Easton directed his answer at Rourke, "Sometimes we do stupid things to protect the people we love." He turned back to Cash. "Before I say anything else I'd like to speak to my lawyer."

"I won't be pressing charges," Rourke said.

"What?" Cash demanded.

"Consider it a wedding present," Rourke said to Easton. "I hope the two of you will be happy."

Easton nodded, eyes shiny. "I'm glad you're back, Rourke. You'll have to give me some tips on staying alive in the Big House."

"For a white-collar crime like cooking your own books?" Rourke said. "A good lawyer can get you off. Now that you're marrying his daughter, I'm sure John Logan knows of a good attorney or two."

Easton smiled and held out his hand. Rourke looked at it for a moment, then shook it.

Cash started to say something but the two-way radio in his patrol car squawked. "Don't move. I'm not finished with you," he said to Rourke and went to answer it.

Through the window, Rourke watched Easton go back inside the office. Blaze looked up, her expression filled with fear. Rourke couldn't hear what was being said but he could guess. Blaze's expression turned to one of disbelief, then shock, then she was crying and Easton was on his knees proposing. Blaze must have said yes, because the next moment, she was in his arms.

"Get in!" Cash called from the patrol car and flipped on his siren.

The car was already rolling as Rourke closed the door.

"It's Cassidy. She got a call from Yvonne. She's gone out there. The dispatcher said Cassidy heard a sound on the line, then the phone was dropped."

Rourke swore and watched the highway as it blurred past. For the first time in years, he prayed for someone other than himself.

As Cassidy pushed on the bathroom door she saw the sink, the mirror over it fogged with condensation. Had Yvonne dropped the phone because she'd forgotten she'd left the water running in the tub?

But then where was she now?

Cassidy caught an acrid wet scent as the door creaked all the way open.

The red shower curtain was drawn across the tub. No water on the floor, but the room was humid as if someone had just taken a bath. Odd. Odd, too, that smell. Like burnt electrical wiring.

She glanced at the red shower curtain, her imagination creeping her out. *Don't. Don't even consider it.*

She'd seen too many horror movies as a teenager. She reached for the curtain to pull it back. That's when she heard it. A siren in the distance. Cash. She breathed a sigh of relief and thought about going downstairs to wait for him.

But her fingers were already on the shower curtain. She drew it back, telling herself later she'd laugh about how scared she was because the tub would be empty, a faint ring around the edge from where the sudsy water had been earlier.

She heard something behind her. A sound like a soft jingle. But her gaze was on the tub.

It wasn't empty.

Cassidy screamed, the sound ricocheting off the walls as the sight branded itself on her brain. Yvonne fully clothed lying in the tub of water. Her face blue and floating just under the surface, legs splayed, knees up. The still-plugged-in hair dryer resting on her chest.

Cassidy swung around, half falling, half lurching back through the bathroom door onto the landing. She heard a sound, a door creaking open. She turned her head.

At first she thought it was Cash, that somehow he'd gotten there quicker than she'd expected. But she could still hear the siren drawing closer and the dark figure came from a now partially opened doorway that had been closed earlier.

She couldn't make out the features in the shadowy darkness of the landing until the figure was almost on top of her. And then it was too late. She didn't have time to react. Didn't even have time to get her arm up.

The blow caught her in the temple, the force knocking her backward. She felt the air rush from her lungs as she fell, then saw nothing but darkness.

Chapter Fourteen

"Cassidy!" Rourke took the stairs three at a time with Cash yelling for him to wait as he ran through the ransacked house.

She was slumped against the wall on the landing, her head tilted to one side. His heart caught in his throat. No! Oh, God no.

But the moment he touched her, he knew she was alive. She stirred and let out a soft moan, her hand going to the bump on her head. Her eyes came open. She focused on him, a smile turning up the corners of her mouth.

"Rourke."

He thought his heart would burst from his chest as he drew her to him. "Are you all right?" he whispered against her hair.

She nodded and rubbed her temple. "He hit me."

"Who?" Cash asked as he reached the landing, his weapon drawn.

Cassidy drew back a little from Rourke's embrace, her eyes widening. "Yvonne." The word came out on a sob as she motioned toward the open bathroom door.

Rourke exchanged a look with Cash, then Cash

stepped into the bathroom, his weapon still drawn. Rourke heard a curse, then Cash checked the other rooms and called for the coroner and forensics crew out of Billings.

"Yvonne's dead," he said, then knelt down close to Cassidy and checked her pupils. "Who hit you, Cassidy?"

"A man. I think I saw his face…." She frowned, then held her head.

"I don't think you have a concussion," Cash said. "How do you feel?"

Rourke was still holding her, never wanting to let her go.

"Woozy but all right. Yvonne said she was at Wild Horse Gulch the night Forrest was killed. She said she went up there to meet him. She saw the murderer leaving on horseback, but didn't recognize him. She was scared because she thought he'd found out about her." Cassidy let out a sob. "Forrest was still alive when she found him that night. He had a medal in his hand, a Saint Christopher medal, the chain broken. He gave it to her."

"The killer's?" Rourke said on a breath.

Cassidy nodded. "That's why she was so afraid. She feared the killer would get her before you found out who he was if he knew she had the medal and had been the woman Forrest was meeting that night."

"Yvonne has been sitting on this for eleven years?" Rourke couldn't believe it.

"She was scared he'd come after her."

"It seems that's exactly what he did," Cash said. "Is anything coming back? Something you might have seen or heard or smelled…."

She shook her head.

"Do you think you can stand?" Rourke asked her. He couldn't remember ever being that frightened. He held Cassidy tightly to him as he helped her up.

"Wait a minute, there was something. I heard a jingle, like change in a pocket or a lot of keys on a ring." She shook her head. "That's all I can remember and I can't even be sure about that. I thought I saw his face, but it's gone now."

"You were hit pretty hard from the size of the knot on your head," Cash said.

"Gavin," she said suddenly. "I thought I heard Gavin's voice when Yvonne left the line before I came out to check on her."

Cash looked startled. "I passed Holt's car as I was coming out. It looked like Gavin behind the wheel. You take Cassidy back to the cabin. I'm going to have a talk with Gavin." Cash took off.

He glanced back at the bathroom. "If only Yvonne had come forward eleven years ago."

A set of dual sirens grew louder and louder as the state boys arrived.

Rourke told them where the sheriff had gone and left word for Cash to call him when he heard something.

Cassidy was quiet on the drive to the cabin. He turned up the heater and wrapped his coat around her, but he could see that she was still shaking.

He drew her to him and she snuggled into him.

"I can't believe this is happening," she whispered against his chest. "I can't believe this."

He wished he couldn't, but he'd known for eleven years that the killer was still out there.

At the cabin, Rourke dug out his father's stash of

good bourbon from where Asa kept it hidden for his fishing trips with Cash.

He poured Cassidy a little in a glass. "Here, drink this."

She downed it, coughed and looked up at him. "What was that?" she said on a single breath.

"The best bourbon money can buy. Asa's good stuff. He swears it will put hair on your chest."

"I hope not."

CASSIDY DIDN'T REALIZE how tense she was until Rourke's cell phone rang and she practically jumped out of her skin. She watched as he answered it, listening to his side of the conversation.

"Yeah? Thanks, Cash. Yeah, I'll tell her. No, she's fine. I will. Okay." He clicked off.

She watched her face. "It's bad, isn't it?"

"Gavin was driving Holt's car. Cash tried to pull him over. Gavin made a run for it and missed that corner down by the coal mine. He's dead."

Cassidy took a breath and let it out as Rourke sat down beside her.

"Gavin had a nasty scratch on his face. The forensics tech found skin and blood under Yvonne's fingernails. Cash is waiting for the results but it looks like Gavin killed Yvonne." He hesitated. "There's more. The forensics tech found a Saint Christopher medal in Gavin's car. The chain had been broken and the silver was tarnished."

Cassidy felt tears burn her eyes. "The one Yvonne told me about."

"Looks that way. It's over, Cassidy. You're safe. And I'm…I'm free."

"Oh, Rourke," she whispered, and began to cry, so filled with emotion. She had prayed for this day. She looked into his wonderful pale blue eyes and felt her heart soar.

He kissed her softly on the lips, then pulled back. "No hiccups?" he asked, smiling at her.

She shook her head, waiting for a moment, then smiled. "Not a one."

He slipped his hand around her waist and drew her to him. His mouth dropped to hers and her lips parted not in surprise but in response to his ardor. Her arms came around his neck, she sighed against his mouth, a satisfied sigh as he wrapped her in his arms.

Cassidy felt as if she'd come home. It was the oddest feeling. Especially given her response to the first kiss. Actually their second. The barn kiss had been quick, a brush of dry lips, but it had jump-started her heart.

Their second kiss had been better, no doubt about that. Her racing heart and her hiccups could attest to that.

But this kiss. Oh, this latest kiss…it was all that she'd dreamed of. Just like being wrapped in Rourke's arms.

She told herself she was dreaming as she listened to the thump-thump of his heart. This couldn't be happening. Dreams like this didn't come true.

He drew back and she thought, well that was that. He would apologize, promise never to do that again and she would hang on to the memory of the kiss for another fifteen years.

But when he looked into her eyes, she felt her heart jackhammer in her chest.

"Cassidy?" he asked in a whisper.

She nodded, not sure what the question was but darn sure of her answer.

He seemed to hesitate, but only for a moment before his mouth lowered to hers again, the kiss slow and sensual. His tongue parted her lips and, as he entered her, she couldn't stop the moan that escaped.

He drew her to him, pressing his body to hers as the kiss deepened. This kiss she could live on the rest of her life.

"Cassidy," he whispered against her mouth as if her name were a prayer.

She locked her arms around his waist as his mouth devoured hers. Her knees seemed to melt and the next thing she knew, he was sweeping her into his arms.

He kicked open the bedroom door and strode in with her. And then they were on the bed and he was kissing her senseless again.

His fingers worked the buttons of her uniform top. She felt the cool breeze caress her skin, then his warm palm. She sucked in a breath as his fingers skimmed over the hard tip of one nipple then the other.

She'd squeezed her eyes closed tight but didn't realize it until he stopped touching her and she opened her eyes, startled to find him above her, looking intently down at her.

"Are you sure about this?" he asked.

Just as sure as she was about taking her next breath. She nodded, wanting to plead with him not to stop. Not now. Not after she'd dreamed of nothing else for years.

His gaze held hers for a long, long moment, then his

mouth dropped to her left breast. She groaned, arching against the warm wetness. Don't stop. Don't ever stop.

He didn't. It was everything she had ever dreamed— and so, so much more.

IT RAINED THAT NIGHT. A soft *tap, tap, tap* on the metal roof that lulled them both to sleep in each other's arms.

It was the first night Rourke had slept in a real bedroom since he'd gotten out of prison or without waking with a start in the middle of the night and feeling disoriented, scared and alone.

He awoke to find Cassidy's face inches from his own, her brown eyes open. Clearly she had been watching him sleep. Something about that seemed more intimate than even their lovemaking the night before.

She smiled at him shyly, tentatively. "Good morning."

"Good morning." He returned her smile. She looked dewy-eyed fresh, uninhibited. He remembered how Blaze had gotten up before him in the mornings, rushing to refresh her makeup as if afraid for him to see her without it.

Cassidy wore no makeup. She always looked fresh and clean, smelling of soap.

This morning she looked as delectable as she had last night, maybe even more so given their new intimacy.

He leaned nearer to gently kiss her. His cell phone rang. He groaned and fished through the pocket of his jacket tossed carelessly on the floor the night before.

"Hello?"

"Rourke, it's Easton. I just heard the news. I'm so

glad that your name is going to be cleared." News traveled faster than the speed of light in Antelope Flats.

"How is Blaze taking the news about Gavin?"

"You know Blaze. She and Gavin were never close. He's always been in some sort of trouble or another. She was surprised that he was capable of killing anyone, though. It's too bad but we're just glad it's over."

"Me, too."

"I don't know if you've heard but Les Thurman is throwing a party tonight at the Mello Dee to celebrate your freedom and announce Blaze's and my engagement. I hope you and Cassidy will come. It would mean a lot to me. And to Blaze. New beginnings?"

Rourke glanced over at Cassidy. They would have all day together before the party tonight. "I'll ask Cassidy." He told her what Easton had said.

"They're engaged?" she whispered. "This I have to see."

"We'll be there." He clicked off.

"It won't bother you to go back to the Mello Dee? It is Saturday night," she said. "Or did you forget about *my* plan?"

He smiled. "That was the worst plan you ever came up with," he joked. It seemed like a million years ago that he'd come up with that crazy idea.

"Rourke, I can't help but wonder why Gavin killed Forrest."

"He and Forrest were involved in something illegal, we know that much, and they had a falling out," Rourke said. "We might never know. I've wondered too how Gavin got my gun." He met Cassidy's gaze. "Blaze. You think she stole it for her stepbrother?"

"Anything is possible, I suppose," Cassidy said slowly. "But they were never close. I find it hard to believe even Blaze would do that."

"Remember this is the same woman who took potshots at us just yesterday," Rourke reminded her as he leaned down to kiss her. "I think Blaze is trying to change, though."

"Right." Men could be so naive sometimes, Cassidy thought.

"I feel like an incredible weight has been lifted from my shoulders. It's over, Cassidy. Now I can start thinking about the future. Speaking of the future…" She smiled and he drew her to him. "We have all day before the party."

"Hmm," she whispered. "All day, huh?"

THE PARKING LOT at the Mello Dee Lounge and Supper Club was packed when Rourke and Cassidy arrived. Rourke spotted his brother's patrol car in the lot. Cash wasn't much of a partygoer so it surprised him.

As they walked in the front door, Cash met them as if he'd been waiting for them. "Cassidy, could you give us a minute?" he asked.

"Cassidy!" Les called. "I heard what happened. The drinks are on the house. What will you have?"

"Go ahead," she said to Rourke. "I'll be fine." She slid onto the bar stool and ordered a light beer.

"You sure you wouldn't like something stronger?" Les asked with a smile.

She shook her head, smiling. She was already intoxicated on life. On Rourke.

"Well, at least let me pour it in a glass for you." Les laughed as he went down the bar to get her beer. Several other bartenders were behind the long bar, serving up drinks to the lively crowd. Music blared from the jukebox and voices tried to talk over the music.

Everyone in town seemed to be here. The tables were full and people were spilling in and out of the larger rooms at the back.

She noticed Blaze and Easton were at the center of it all. Blaze saw her, whispered something to Easton and headed her way.

Cassidy groaned inwardly. It was one thing to celebrate her cousin's engagement, it was another to actually be forced to talk to her. Was that why Cash had wanted to talk to Rourke, because he'd discovered that Blaze had stolen Rourke's gun, which her stepbrother used to kill Forrest?

"Cassidy, I'm so glad you came tonight," Blaze said. "There is something I need to say to you."

Cassidy braced herself.

"I'm sorry."

Sorry? Cassidy couldn't help her surprise.

"I've always resented the hell out of you," Blaze said with a laugh. "In truth, I wanted to be you." She laughed again. "That's not going to happen so I'm just trying to deal with being me."

Cassidy was speechless.

"I'm really happy about you and Rourke. That's the way it should have always been. If I hadn't messed things up for you years ago…"

Cassidy was shaking her head. "Rourke and I aren't—"

"Maybe things worked out for the best, you know? Rourke has changed and that's good." Someone began to make a toast to the lucky couple. "Anyway, I'm sorry. I'd better get back to Easton."

"Congratulations," Cassidy managed to say before Blaze left. She stared after her in shock. Had Blaze really said she'd always wanted to be her and that she was sorry?

Les put her beer down in front of her at the end of the bar and she took a drink. "How is it?" he asked.

"Great. Thanks."

"So Gavin killed Yvonne and Forrest?" Les asked, shaking his head in disbelief.

"Looks that way. I'm just glad that it's over."

"You all right? I heard Yvonne Ames's place was ransacked and you were the one to find her."

She nodded, not letting herself remember what she'd found behind the shower curtain.

"Any idea what Gavin was looking for?"

She hesitated, not sure how much of what she knew was public knowledge. She shook her head and took a sip of beer.

Les was watching her closely, as if he knew she wasn't telling him everything. Les was worse than a hairdresser when it came to wanting all the good gossip.

"So Yvonne saw Gavin kill Forrest?" he asked.

"We may never know."

"Too bad all this didn't come out eleven years ago at the trial," he said. "Could have saved Rourke a lot of heartache."

She nodded.

"I wonder why Yvonne called you? I didn't realize the two of you were friends," Les said.

"She'd heard that I was helping Rourke look for the real killer."

Les was shaking his head. "All these years she never said a word. Who would have known? How's your head? I heard you got hit pretty hard. You didn't see Gavin hit you?"

"No, I…" Again she hesitated. She could see the dark hallway, someone coming toward her, remembered thinking it was Cash, then realizing it couldn't be Cash.

"You remember something?" he asked.

She shook her head and smiled. "I feel like it's just right there, like on the tip of my brain."

He glanced at her beer glass. "Drink up. I'll make you something special that's bound to help you remember."

Cassidy took another sip of her beer as Les went down to the other end of the bar to make her drink. She wondered what was keeping Rourke and Cash.

ROURKE DIDN'T LIKE leaving Cassidy alone. Not because he was worried about her anymore. He just liked being with her. "What's so important we have to do this now?"

"Forensics found something that doesn't make any sense," Cash said, once he and Rourke were outside the bar and away from earshot. "Yvonne had had sex right before she was killed."

Rourke stared at him in shock. "You aren't going to tell me—"

"Gavin's DNA was found inside her."

"Was she raped?"

Cash was shaking his head.

"What the hell?" Rourke said, pacing in a tight circle. "She had sex with him and then he put her clothes back on and drowned her in the tub?"

"They could have had a lovers' quarrel afterward, after they were both dressed," Cash suggested.

"A man who's worried that she's going to talk and get him sent to prison for murder isn't going to make love to her first," Rourke snapped. "You're telling me he might not be the killer."

"I talked to one neighbor," Cash said. "This wasn't the first time Gavin spent time at Yvonne's. It seems they were lovers. The neighbor also heard them fighting a lot. One time, Yvonne had a black eye the next day. That could explain the scratches this time."

Rourke swore and looked toward the Mello Dee. "Gavin didn't kill her."

"Then why did he run when I tried to pull him over?" Cash said.

"Guilty conscience over something else maybe."

Cash nodded. "I talked to Holt VanHorn, asked him why Gavin was driving his car. He broke down and told me that Gavin had been blackmailing him." He sighed. "Holt admitted to stealing the murder weapon from your bedroom the night of your birthday party."

Rourke swore.

"Holt swears the gun was stolen out of his car and he doesn't know who killed Forrest," Cash said. "It looks like the killer is still out there."

LES RETURNED to Cassidy at the end of the bar, laughing at some joke someone had told him. He had a drink for her in his hand. "Come here," he said, motioning for her to follow him.

She took a quick glance toward the room full of people. Everyone was gathered around Easton and Blaze. She looked toward the door. Rourke and Cash must still be outside talking.

"You've got to hear this," Les said, motioning her toward the hallway to the back door.

She slid off the stool, feeling woozy. She hardly ever drank. The beer had gone to her head. Or she was still unsteady from the blow she'd taken yesterday. She started down the short narrow hallway toward the back of the Mello Dee.

"Easy," Les said, suddenly at her side.

"I just need a little air."

"Here, let me help you. You don't look so good." He led her down the hallway, the music and voices growing dimmer. As he walked beside her, his keys jingled softly. She tried to remember where she'd heard that sound, but her brain seemed fuzzy and she could barely lift her feet.

"Where are you taking…"

"Just need to cool you off," he said, and opened the large walk-in beer cooler. He shoved her in before she could react. She stumbled and fell to her knees. The door closed with a soft whoosh.

She turned as she grabbed a shelf and pulled herself up to her feet. Her legs felt like water. She had to lean against the shelf full of cases of beer and wine. Her mouth felt cottony and she could see her breath when she breathed. Les seemed to waver in front of her like heat waves on pavement in the hot summer sun.

"What are you doing?" Her voice sounded funny. But her brain was still working, just too slowly. "You put something in my beer." She opened her mouth to scream.

"Don't bother screaming. The walls are too thick. Even if the music wasn't so loud, no one would hear you."

Her scream died before it made it to her throat. She swallowed, her mouth so dry she could barely talk let alone scream.

"You saw me, didn't you," Les said.

She tried to focus on him, focus on his words.

"You looked right at me. I knew I should have finished you right then, but I could hear that damned siren." He was shaking his head.

"It was *you* in the hallway at Yvonne's?"

"Right on the tip of your brain, huh? At the café, I heard you on the phone with Yvonne, heard what you said about Wild Horse Gulch and the mystery woman Forrest had called. Everyone thought it was Blaze."

Cassidy shivered as his words registered. The cold air in the cooler was already working its way to her bones and she felt sick and weak.

"The back door of Yvonne's house was open," Les continued as if talking more to himself. "I heard Gavin upstairs with her, the radio blaring, the two of them fighting, then making love. I knew Yvonne had no imagination if she was doing Gavin, so it was easy to figure out where she would hide my Saint Christopher medal. I knew I had to tie up all of the loose ends." He took a breath. "I put the medal in the car Gavin was driving, then I waited for him to leave. The problem was he came back a second time. He'd forgotten his hat. He saw Yvonne in the tub and freaked." Les laughed. "Serves the worthless puke right. Beating up women."

He abhorred beating up women, but he'd killed Yvonne? And Forrest?

He rubbed a hand over his face. His words came out in puffs of white. "I thought Forrest was dead, then he made a grab for me. I could hear the car coming up the road. Any moment I'd be caught in the headlights. I tried to pry his fingers loose from the chain, but there wasn't time."

Cassidy fought to stay awake. She could feel the effects of the drug coursing through her system. If she fell asleep in here, she'd die of hypothermia.

"I didn't stick around. That property used to be mine before Mason VanHorn cheated me out of it. I knew every inch of it. Forrest couldn't have picked a better spot. He never expected anyone to come by horseback."

Les seemed lost in his story, as if he'd needed to tell someone and now he had a captive audience. She couldn't move. Feared if she tried to take a step her legs would fail her.

"I just assumed the vehicle coming up the road was Rourke's. Or Blaze. I'd hoped my Saint Christopher medal was lost in the rain that night when it didn't turn up."

She mouthed one word. "Why?"

He seemed surprised she could still talk. "Why? That bastard Forrest was blackmailing me. He'd seen me vandalize Mason VanHorn's coal-bed methane wells. He was bleeding me dry. Mason knew about the methane on my land. He knew I was losing the place, he offered me pennies on the dollar for my land, then made a fortune. So I destroyed a few of his precious wells out of spite and I knew it was just a matter of time before Forrest gave me up and collected the reward Mason was offering. I had no choice but to kill him."

The words she muttered were almost indistinguishable. "Rourke's gun."

Les must have been anticipating the question. "I stole it out of the back of Holt VanHorn's rig, thinking I'd get back at Mason when his son was arrested for murder. I had no idea it wasn't Holt's gun. I was sick when it turned out to be Rourke's. I could have killed Holt."

Les looked at his watch as if worried he'd been gone too long. Surely he wouldn't leave her here to die. He stripped off his belt and came toward her.

She tried to dodge him, but her legs gave way. Her fingers clasped the front of his shirt as she fell. She heard the tinkle of buttons hitting the cold floor, heard him let out an oath.

He was on her at once, using the belt to tie her to a metal shelf. Her teeth chattered. She licked her lips, tried to form the words. "Don't...Les."

"I'm sorry, Cassidy. If Gavin hadn't come back, I wouldn't have been trapped in the bedroom, I wouldn't have had to hit you, you wouldn't have seen me." He shook his head. "I never wanted any of this. But I couldn't take the chance you would remember seeing me."

She pulled against the restraints as he rose to his feet. She was too weak to pull free. She watched him push open the door. She tried to scream, but nothing came out, then Les was gone, taking a case of beer with him. The door closed and she was alone, freezing cold and scared she would never see Rourke again.

ROURKE RUSHED BACK into the Mello Dee, fear tightening his insides the moment he saw the empty stool at the end of the bar where Cassidy had been sitting.

"Have you seen Cassidy?" he asked as he moved through the bar. No one had.

He got Les's attention.

"Cassidy?" Les asked over the din. "Ladies' rest room?"

Rourke started to head for the opposite end of the bar where the rest rooms were found when he noticed that Les's shirt was open, the buttons missing. He frowned. A memory from a night Rourke had spent eleven years trying to forget. Les breaking up the fight between him and Forrest. A flicker of light, something cool swinging down and touching his cheek as Les bent over him and separated him and Forrest.

"You used to wear a Saint Christopher medal."

Les met his gaze. "What?"

"What happened to the buttons on your shirt, Les?"

Les reached down and Rourke knew before he lifted his hand that the bartender was going for the baseball bat he kept behind the bar.

Before Les could swing it, Rourke grabbed Les by the arm and dragged him over the bar.

"Kill the jukebox," Rourke yelled as Cash appeared next to him.

In the next instant, the music stopped and Cash was yelling for everyone to be quiet.

"Where is Cassidy?" Rourke was yelling down at

Les. "Tell me where she is. If you hurt one hair on her head—"

"I saw her follow Les down the hallway toward the back of the bar," someone called from the crowd.

Rourke released Les and ran down the hallway. There were only two doors. A storage room. He jerked open the door. No Cassidy. And the beer cooler. He pulled open the heavy door, a gust of cold coming out.

He saw her huddled against one of the shelves. "Cassidy, oh God, Cassidy."

Her eyes fluttered open and her lips formed a lopsided smile. "My hero," she mouthed.

He hurriedly untied the belt and swept her up in his arms, rushing her from the cooler.

"Blankets," Easton yelled.

"There's one in my car," Blaze said, and ran outside.

Moments later Rourke had Cassidy wrapped in a blanket, in his arms. All the years he'd repressed his anger, he'd also repressed his emotions. But one emotion threatened to drown him as he looked down at her.

"I love you, Cassidy," he whispered as he pressed his cheek against hers, then pulled back to look into her eyes. "I came home bitter and angry. All I wanted was revenge. Against you. But once I got to know you…" He shook his head. "You are an amazing woman, Ms. Miller. I can't imagine life without you in it."

Cash took Les into custody and searched the bar, finding the drug he'd used to dope Cassidy. "She's going to be all right. Doc says it will just wear off. But if you hadn't found her when you did, she would have died of hypothermia."

Rourke took her to the closest place he knew of—the Siesta Motel—and got her into the shower with him. It didn't take long to warm her up. He seemed to have a talent for it.

"I love you, Rourke McCall," she whispered. "Do you realize how many years I've waited to say that?"

Epilogue

Cassidy woke to the smell of bacon. She opened her eyes. Rourke stood over her holding a tray.

"Hungry?"

She was, she realized, as she sat up and he placed the tray on her lap and sat down on the side of the bed.

He'd taken her to his family ranch. Rourke's mother had insisted the guest room be prepared for her.

"I was going to put her in my room," Rourke said.

Shelby had given him a look. "Cassidy doesn't want to be in any bed you've shared with another woman, no matter how many years ago it was. Don't you know anything about women?"

"No, but I'm trying to learn," Rourke said.

Cassidy had laughed.

"Now get," Shelby had said to her son last night. "The girl needs her rest."

Rourke left and Shelby smiled down at her. "I know we've never met, but I've heard wonderful things about you," the older woman said. "I couldn't be happier about having you here. Now, you get some rest. If you need anything, you just press that button, all right?"

"Thank you," Cassidy said. She'd closed her eyes, wondering if she'd only dreamed the part where Rourke had said he loved her and she'd said she loved him.

"How did you sleep?" he asked now. Sunlight streamed in the windows, the day bright.

"Good," she said, and realized it was true.

"Eat up, you'll need your strength. The rest of the family is anxious to see you." He handed her a piece of toast with a strip of bacon on top.

She took a bite and looked at Rourke. She felt shy around him. Did he regret telling her he'd loved her? If he really had. "I don't remember much from last night."

"You remember Les drugging you?" he asked.

She nodded. "And I remember most of what he told me in the cooler about Forrest blackmailing him over the coal-bed methane wells Les had sabotaged on the VanHorn Ranch. Les took the gun out of Holt's car, thinking it was Holt's, and killed Forrest."

Rourke nodded, and picked up a piece of bacon, eating it before saying, "He's made a full confession to Cash. He killed Yvonne once he realized she had his Saint Christopher medal. He was afraid she'd seen him as he was leaving, after killing Forrest. It was like a house of cards, once it began to fall. Cash arrested Holt. He's confessed to stealing my gun at the birthday party. I'm sure he'll get off. Mason will hire the best lawyers money can buy."

"Is it really over?" she asked.

"Yes." He touched her check with his fingertips and gazed into her eyes. "It's really over." He moved the tray and pulled her into his arms.

"Ahem," came a familiar voice from the doorway.

"Let her eat and get a shower. We're all waiting downstairs," Shelby ordered, then left.

Rourke laughed. "Looks like she's not only staying, she'd ordering everyone around, even Asa, but amazingly he's taking it." He shook his head as if he didn't understand it at all. He rose from the bed and smiled down at her. "See you downstairs?"

Cassidy nodded.

She showered, finding everything she needed along with some of her own clothing, which Rourke had brought from her house. After brushing her hair, she dressed and went down the wide stairway to find Rourke was right. The entire family was waiting.

They all greeted her, but it was Rourke who got to his feet and met her on the bottom step. He looked a little nervous and she wondered why he'd been so insistent about her staying at the ranch for a while.

"Cassidy," he said, and dug into his jacket pocket. "There's something I want to ask you."

She glanced toward his mother. Shelby was nodding, her eyes brimming with tears.

"Will you marry me? I promise to make you a good husband. I'll love you and cherish you and take care of you—"

"Give her a chance to answer," Asa said. Everyone laughed.

Rourke produced a small jewelry box from his pocket. "I love you, Cassidy."

She stared at him. It hadn't been a dream.

"Help me out here, Cassidy," he whispered. "Please, say you'll marry me. I know it's sudden but—"

"Yes. Oh yes," she said, and threw her arms around

him, then she opened the small dark velvet box. A beautiful diamond ring twinkled up at her.

Rourke took it out and slipped it on her finger. She stared down at it, then at him. She'd imagined this since the age of thirteen and she couldn't have imagined it being more wonderful.

The family rushed to the two of them with congratulations and hugs and tears. Asa offered Rourke land up the road to build a house on and asked him to come back to the ranch. When Rourke looked to her, Cassidy nodded her approval.

He kept his arm around her, his gaze often meeting hers, as they all talked about the future.

Maybe someday she'd even let him read the letters she'd written him while he was in prison.

ROURKE HAD NEVER appreciated his family as much as he did at that moment. He loved them. And, he realized just how much he'd missed them, warts and all. That's why he'd brought Cassidy here, that's why he wanted to ask her to marry him with his family around them.

"I've decided to go to law school," Brandon announced. "I wasn't cut out for ranch work. I want to be a lawyer."

There were groans all around.

"This family could use a good lawyer," Brandon argued. "One of us is always in trouble."

Asa patted his son on the back. "If that's what you want, then do it."

They all looked at Asa as if they'd never seen him before. He'd been a different man since Shelby had returned. Rourke still suspected there was more to the story, but Asa and Shelby weren't telling it.

"*I* could use some help around the ranch," J.T. said disagreeably.

"Well, Asa isn't going to be helping," Shelby said, coming to stand by her husband's side. She took his hand. "He and I need to spend some time together and he's worked this ranch long enough."

"Don't look at *me*. Cassidy and I are going on a long honeymoon," Rourke said. "I'm thinking something tropical."

Cassidy smiled and nodded. "Sounds heavenly."

"You have to get married first," Dusty spoke up. She'd been pretty quiet since Shelby's return. Of all the kids, she was the one who hadn't forgiven her mother or father.

"Will you help me plan my wedding?" Cassidy asked her.

Dusty's eyes lit up. "Really?"

"I'm going to need a lot of help," Cassidy said. "And I'm going to need a maid of honor."

"*Really?* I have some magazines," Dusty said, then flushed when everyone looked at her. "I was just *looking* at them." As far as Rourke knew, Dusty wasn't dating. But the neighbor boy, Ty Coltrane had been coming around a lot, making excuses, always looking for Dusty and trying to get her attention when he found her. She didn't seem to notice.

"I suppose you heard that my camp cook broke his leg trying to ride some mechanical bull down in Cheyenne," J.T. complained. He really did need a woman, Rourke thought.

"Buck'll find you a cook before you go up to bring the cattle down from summer pasture," Asa said.

"I hate to imagine what Buck will come up with," J.T. grumbled. Buck Brannigan had been the ranch foreman since Rourke was a boy. He was a crusty old character who grumbled more than J.T. A loner, he stayed up the road in the original homestead cabin and wasn't much help anymore, but a definite permanent fixture at the Sundown Ranch.

"When is this wedding going to be?" Shelby asked.

Rourke looked at Cassidy. "As soon as possible."

She laughed and nodded. "Can we put together a wedding in the next two weeks?" she asked Dusty.

Dusty's eyes were as big as saucers. "There is so much to do. Flowers, food for the reception, everyone in town will want to come, and a cake and a dress…"

Cassidy looked to Shelby. "Will you help, too?"

Shelby glanced at her daughter. "Would you mind?"

Dusty shrugged. "I guess not."

"Great," Cassidy said. She couldn't wait to be Rourke's wife.

"J.T., can you wait to go up into the high country until after the wedding?" Rourke asked. "I want to see you in a tux as one of my three best men."

Rourke pulled his wife-to-be closer and wondered what he'd done in life to deserve this woman. Nothing, he thought. He'd just gotten lucky. And he would never forget it.

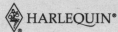
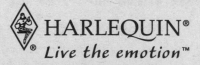

Like a phantom in the night comes
a new promotion from

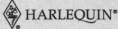
HARLEQUIN®

INTRIGUE®

GOTHIC ROMANCE

Beginning in August 2004, we offer you
a classic blend of chilling suspense and
electrifying romance, starting with....

A DANGEROUS INHERITANCE
LEONA KARR

And don't miss a spine-tingling Eclipse tale each month!

September 2004
MIDNIGHT ISLAND SANCTUARY
SUSAN PETERSON

October 2004
THE LEGACY OF CROFT CASTLE
JEAN BARRETT

November 2004
THE MAN FROM FALCON RIDGE
RITA HERRON

December 2004
EDEN'S SHADOW
JENNA RYAN

Available wherever Harlequin books are sold.
www.eHarlequin.com   HIECLIPSE

If you enjoyed what you just read,
then we've got an offer you can't resist!

Take 2 bestselling love stories FREE!

Plus get a FREE surprise gift!

Clip this page and mail it to Harlequin Reader Service®

IN U.S.A.	**IN CANADA**
3010 Walden Ave.	P.O. Box 609
P.O. Box 1867	Fort Erie, Ontario
Buffalo, N.Y. 14240-1867	L2A 5X3

YES! Please send me 2 free Harlequin Intrigue® novels and my free surprise gift. After receiving them, if I don't wish to receive anymore, I can return the shipping statement marked cancel. If I don't cancel, I will receive 4 brand-new novels each month, before they're available in stores! In the U.S.A., bill me at the bargain price of $4.24 plus 25¢ shipping and handling per book and applicable sales tax, if any*. In Canada, bill me at the bargain price of $4.99 plus 25¢ shipping and handling per book and applicable taxes**. That's the complete price and a savings of at least 10% off the cover prices—what a great deal! I understand that accepting the 2 free books and gift places me under no obligation ever to buy any books. I can always return a shipment and cancel at any time. Even if I never buy another book from Harlequin, the 2 free books and gift are mine to keep forever.

181 HDN DZ7N
381 HDN DZ7P

Name	(PLEASE PRINT)	
Address	Apt.#	
City	State/Prov.	Zip/Postal Code

Not valid to current Harlequin Intrigue® subscribers.

Want to try two free books from another series?
Call 1-800-873-8635 or visit www.morefreebooks.com.

* Terms and prices subject to change without notice. Sales tax applicable in N.Y.
** Canadian residents will be charged applicable provincial taxes and GST.
   All orders subject to approval. Offer limited to one per household.
   ® are registered trademarks owned and used by the trademark owner and or its licensee.

INT04R   ©2004 Harlequin Enterprises Limited

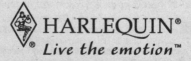